FREEDOM'S EDGE

An American Trilogy

A Story of America's War for Independence in the South:
The People Who Fought and Won, and Those Who Fought and Lost

Jill LaForge Jones

Book Three
FIGHTING FOR TOMORROW

Also by the Author

Written as Jill Jones:
Emily's Secret
My Lady Caroline
The Scottish Rose
Essence of My Desire (retitled A Scent of Magic)
Circle of the Lily
The Island
Bloodline
Remember Your Lies
Every Move You Make

Written as Emily LaForge:
Beneath the Ravens' Moon
Shadow Haven

AUTHOR BIO

Jill LaForge Jones is the award-winning author of eleven novels of romance and suspense. She holds a bachelor's degree in Journalism with emphasis on Professional Writing from the University of Oklahoma where she graduated Magna Cum Laude and was inducted into Phi Beta Kappa. She has written for a wide variety of audiences and media, including print, audio, video, and online content. During the last twenty years, she served as director of the Swannanoa Valley Museum in Black Mountain, NC, and director of Marketing & Communications for the Blue Ridge National Heritage Area, work in which she traveled throughout the region and learned about the unique history and culture of western North Carolina.

This is a work of fiction. Although some characters are historical figures, and some incidents are true to history, other names, characters, places, and incidents are either the product of the author's imagination or used fictitiously.
ISBN– 9780967697277 Paperback
ISBN– 9780967697284 Epub

Cover and book design by Russell Shuler.

AUTHOR'S NOTE

When I was growing up, the history taught in school about America's war for independence was generally depicted through a lens of northern action—the Boston Tea Party, Lexington and Concord, Paul Revere's midnight ride, creation of the Declaration of Independence in Philadelphia, George Washington and Valley Forge, etc. As a student, I was given the impression that the whole thing was relatively simple, based on the "taxation without representation" issue, freedom of religion, and the desire of early immigrants for affordable land.

While all this is true, the picture is far more complex, and it leaves out entire cultures of the natives of the land who were not only disenfranchised by the white man's encroachment, but also came perilously close to extinction. It leaves out the story of the immigrants who forged their new lives in the South—primarily South and North Carolina—and who played a significant role in the eventual defeat of Cornwallis. And it fails to depict the complexity of the relations between white and red man, between a culture with superior technology and one still in the stone age (think guns vs. bow and arrow, steel knives vs. stone spear points.) The story fails to show how over time, the natives' desire to own that technology, partly in self-defense, and to trade with the British for their weapons, manufactured goods, and even trinkets led them to concede land through treaties that many times were ignored or broken. In spite of this, the Cherokee were allies of the British in the War for Independence, and as such met defeat as well.

As a twenty-first century white female, it is difficult to imagine life on this southern frontier between 1750-1780. Who were these immigrants who came into places like Charleston and Wilmington rather than the more typical points of entry such as Philadelphia and New York? Why did they come? What were they running to? Or from? Did they come of their own accord, or were they indentured or enslaved? How bad was life where they came from that they would risk everything and face the unknown in a land rich with promise but rife with danger?

And what of those who already lived on that land? Natives whose ancestors had been there for thousands of years? What did they make of these newcomers? And what part did they play in the white man's war for independence?

Immigration and the problems inherent in the process have been part of the history of mankind since the beginning of time: One tribe wants the land of another, and so will take it by force or cunning. Or one tribe builds a wall to keep another tribe from entering its land. Or tribes unite through marriage or treaty only to fall apart again through treachery or betrayal. It is a never-ending saga of humankind.

My quest is not to resolve this eternal issue, but rather through this work of historical fiction provide the reader with insight into the incredible complexities that faced both the immigrants who came into the southern ports of the British colonies in the mid-eighteenth century and the natives already upon these shores. I have tried to remain true to historic dates and figures, but this is fiction, life imagined in a time and place over two and a half centuries ago, and history sometimes gets fuzzy—in my research, I sometimes encountered different versions of events, times, and places. I have chosen the ones that best fit my story.

My "tribes" are primarily the British, Irish, Highland Scots, Africans, and the Cherokee, descendants of all of which can be found in the mountains and valleys of western North and South Carolina and northern Georgia today. Other "contributing tribes" include the French, Moravians, Scots-Irish, Germans, Swiss, and the Catawba, Shawnee and Creek Indians. The mountains and foothills of North and South Carolina became home to a stew of humanity from both sides of the Atlantic and both hemispheres, brought together by hope, despair, fear, greed, desire for power, lust for land, and that ultimate and elusive aspiration, freedom.

This trilogy is dedicated to those keepers of history in small museums throughout our country, specifically those in western North Carolina, and to the Blue Ridge National Heritage Area.

CHAPTER ONE

Along the Watauga River, North Carolina, February 1771

The day was bleak, gray, and cold with a wet snow starting to fall as Aidan Cassidy Gordon made his way through the forest, looking for a likely place to camp along the river. He'd been on his solitary journey for several months now since leaving Hillsborough, and he was feeling his loneliness. Back at home, he'd heard the tales of the "long hunters," the rough frontiersmen who'd returned from a year or longer in the wilderness on their hunting expeditions and found them compelling. It had been his intent to become one of them, and maybe he still would, but this night, he wished he had more of a companion than his horse. He wasn't sure, but he thought it might be his birthday.

At first, his newfound freedom was exhilarating. He'd left in early fall and enjoyed the warm days and crisp nights and the blazing colors of the trees turning a thousand different shades of red, yellow, and orange. And then the leaves fell, and the trees lay barren and gray, sticks in the air, fallen leaves slick on the forest floor. The air turned from crisp to cool and then to cold. The winds in the high mountains were fierce, biting the flesh and letting the cold seep deep inside.

He'd managed to shoot the deer he needed for survival, and he'd cleaned as many hides as he could carry on the back of his horse in hopes of trading them for future supplies. He'd come across some isolated farms along his way, but nothing that resembled a village or settlement. People had told him about a place called Watauga, and he was headed there now, or at least he hoped so. The Indian part of him didn't want to admit it, but he was a little lost.

He'd heard that the Wataugans were settlers from Virginia and parts of North Carolina who'd grown both weary and wary of English rule, who'd defied the British treaty with the Indians and crossed over into Cherokee territory and settled there. Their settlement was somewhere along this river. When he found them, he hoped he could trade his deer hides to replenish his ammunition, buy a new gun, and resupply for his next foray into the wilderness.

A thin trail of smoke rising just beyond the next ridge caught his eye, and he took his well-used rifle in hand. He'd learned you could never be sure if people you encountered in this wilderness would be friend or foe. He'd met up with a few of both, Cherokees who attacked him for hunting on their lands, and a white trader who stole the first few of his deer hides after pretending to be friendly, even sharing Cass's evening meal before making off with his pelts.

The Cherokees he'd handled by speaking their language and identifying himself as being from Echoe.

Identifying himself. That was the problem.

He'd left home and come on this journey partly to try and find himself. Who was he? Was he white? Cherokee? Irish? English? His mother refused to speak of his blood father, other than to say that he was dead. She'd never told Cass who the man was, or how she came to be his wife, or even where they'd lived, except to say it was in South Carolina. Her real story remained a mystery to him—he knew there was much she hadn't told him, maybe never would.

He'd grown up knowing Indian ways, and the Cherokee ways of living off the land had served him well these past few months. Even now, when he looked up at the stars, he felt closer than ever to the man who had raised him from a tiny baby until the day an English bullet had taken his life. And then there was Will Gordon, who spoke English but with a strong accent, which he had been told was the dialect of the Highlanders of Scotland. Will had been kind to him and tried to be like a father, but he'd found it hard in his mind and his heart to replace his Cherokee father with a white man.

And yet his own skin was white, his hair red, much like Will's only brighter in color. His life in the white man's world had been tolerable, but only just. His mother had tried to school him in reading and writing, but he'd much preferred the education to be had from nature in the woodlands near their home. He cared not a fig for farming, but he did learn some blacksmithing skills from Will. Somehow, though, he just didn't fit there.

And then there was the thing about his name. His mother had named him Aidan, after her own father, but it wasn't a name he much liked. He had been called Firehead by Onacona and the others in the village. In Cherokee ways, women kept their own clan names even after marriage, and Fiona had kept the name of her Irish Cassidy family and gave it to him. But when she married Will Gordon, and he legally adopted her children, he became Aidan Cassidy Gordon. It all seemed overmuch to him. As he pondered these things during the months he'd been in the wilderness, he'd decided to follow the Cherokee tradition of changing one's name when the situation warranted and landed on Cass as a name sufficient for his needs.

He made his way up over the ridge, and looking down into the valley below, he saw a small cabin in a clearing from whence the smoke arose. It was almost dark, and he'd found no suitable camping spot, so he decided to risk it and see if he might take shelter here. A wagon stood beneath a large tree near the house, a horse tethered to the tree, covered with a blanket. This was not the dwelling of an Indian. Maybe he was getting close to the Wataugans.

Cass's horse whinnied when they approached the cabin, announcing their arrival, and a man with a grizzled beard opened the door, the barrel of his shotgun emerging before his body.

"Who goes there?" he called out.

Cass drew his horse to a halt. "A friend. Don't shoot. Name's Cass. Traveling to Watauga. Might you have a place for me to warm my bones on this cold night?"

Never lowering his gun, the man instructed him to tie his horse to the tether rope next to his own horse and come into the cabin. Before doing so, Cass took the bundle of deerskins from the horse and toted them over his shoulder into the warmth of the tiny abode. He'd made a mistake trusting that trader fellow early on in his journey, and he wasn't about to lose sight of these skins.

"What say your name was again?" the man asked as he came through the door.

"You can just call me Cass."

The man studied him a moment, then replied, "All right, then. My name's Greenlee. You can call me Hiram. Come inside before this danged wind blows us away."

Cass stepped into the cabin and was grateful for the warmth, although the wind had found holes in the chinks between the logs and whistled its way inside. He became aware of a figure silhouetted in front of the fireplace. A woman had her back to him, so he couldn't see her face, but her hair was long and plaited down her back, Indian style.

An iron pot hung above the fire, and Hiram Greenlee latched the door behind Cass and went to stir what was cooking in it. Whatever it was, it smelled heavenly to Cass, who hadn't eaten much except fish and venison in the past few months. Something about the scent reminded him of his childhood in his mother's small log cabin in Echoe.

"Won'tcha stash your bundle there in the corner and sit a bit?" Greenlee offered a chair by the fire. Reluctantly Cass placed the bundle in a corner where he could keep an eye on it.

Greenlee saw his look and laughed. "No worries, lad. I won't be stealin' your goods. I'm a trader myself. I know how hard it is to come by such skins. You alone in these woods?"

Cass had to weigh whether to trust this man, and yet he figured he had no good options. "Just me and my horse," he answered, taking a seat and casting a glance at the stewing kettle. Only then did he turn to see the face of the woman who'd remained silent since he'd entered the cabin. At first, he thought his eyes deceived him, or that it was a fancy of his imagination, but he thought he recognized those high cheekbones and long, straight nose. Her hair was almost solid white, and her ruddy skin was wizened and wrinkled.

"Quella?"

CHAPTER TWO

"**Y**ou have come, Firehead, as Onacona told me you would one day." The woman's voice was deep and gravelly, and when she turned to him, Cass saw that her eyes were clouded over with a deep white film. She was likely blind, but she knew him.

Cass was overcome with shock and disbelief. He'd been but a young boy the last time he'd seen Quella, his grandmother's sister who'd often visited Fiona and stayed in their cabin in Echoe. And yet even so young, he knew he'd never forget her. There had always been something strange and magical about her, and he could feel it now. She also carried a distinctive scent, an essence of flowers and smoke, a scent that now filled his senses.

"It is me, Quella. I am Firehead." With that he reached out and took her thin, fragile hands in his large, sturdy ones. "I...I never thought I would see you again."

She smiled and gently stroked the back of his hand. "I knew you would come to me before I made my passing. Onacona told me so in a dream."

"You saw him? He spoke to you?"

Quella only nodded. Cass waited for her to go on, eager to hear what Onacona might have said to her, but the silence in the room was broken only by the gurgle of the stew pot on the fire. Unable to stand the suspense, he asked, "Well, what did he say to you?"

She suppressed a small laugh. "You always were the impatient one, little Firehead. Had a bit of a temper too, as I recall."

At this Hiram Greenlee cleared his throat, reminding them he was in the room. "Shall I bring your burgoo, Quella?"

Again, she just nodded and fell silent. Cass watched as the old trader ladled a small portion of steaming turnips and potatoes with a few chunks of meat into a flat-bottomed tin bowl.

Cass's mouth watered, but he didn't speak. Greenlee pulled up a stool next to Quella, and slowly, in small bites which he blew on to cool, he spooned her dinner into her mouth.

Cass was touched by the gentleness with which the crusty old man fed her. He'd heard stories about traders whose behavior was nothing short of loathsome, stealing from one another, sometimes killing someone in the process. But this man didn't fit that mold at all, and he began to relax. He didn't think Hiram Greenlee would harm him, nor steal his stash of deer hides.

As he fed her, Hiram asked Cass, "Where do you hail from, son, and how did you end up on this cold, stormy night in the high mountains all alone?"

Cass sensed that Quella was all ears even though she didn't speak, so he decided to tell her what had happened to his family after Onacona died. "It was the second year of the British attacks. We were camped out, hiding from the redcoats, when a man came upon our fire," he told them. "We were afraid at first, but we learned he was not one of them, even though he'd served in their army for a short while."

"He killed some of our people," Quella stated suddenly but quietly.

"He said some of your people killed his wife and her family." Cass found himself defending Will. "He was angry and sought revenge by joining the British army for a raid on the Middle Towns. This he told me," he added, reverting to a storytelling technique he'd learned from Onacona.

"But he didn't want to kill," Quella said, as if picking up the thread of his story in her own mind. "And so he left them."

This didn't surprise Cass. Quella had always been able to see things others could not.

"Yes. He'd left them and was on his way back east to where his daughter and friends lived. He said he wanted no more of the frontier. His name was, still is I hope, Will Gordon."

"I know a Will Gordon," Greenlee said, standing and taking the dish to a bowl of water to rinse it out. "Lived on a farm out near Salisbury. Last time I went by there the place was deserted."

"That is him," Cass said, thinking it remarkable how small the community of people was even in this vast land.

"You say his wife and family was kilt by Indians?"

Cass told them the sad tale that Will had finally confided to him. "Only he, his daughter Jeannette, and his sister-in-law Mary, survived that massacre because they weren't there when the Indians attacked."

Greenlee ladled up another serving of the savory stew and handed it and a spoon to Cass. "Here. This'll warm your bones. Mighty sorry to hear about his family."

"Jeannette," Quella said. "That was the baby's name."

"What baby do you speak of?" Hiram asked her, filling a plate for himself.

"The one you told me about, years ago. I delivered that baby myself. What a cold night that was."

"Well, I'll be danged," Greenlee exclaimed.

Cass had never heard the story about the night Jeannette had been born, but it seemed to him as if his world had come full circle when he learned that Quella had been the midwife at that birthing. Quella had also been there when Maura was born. And now Jeannette and Maura were sisters. A wave of emotion rushed over him, and he suddenly missed his Ma and Will and the girls, missed them terribly. He thought he might cry, so he took a large bite of the stew and chewed it hard, managing to swallow it over the tightness in his throat.

"Nanyeh loved you and your mother," the old woman went on. "As did Onacona, my nephew. It is sad so many have died, on both sides."

This did nothing to assuage the grief that threatened Cass's composure. "I loved Nanyeh and Onacona as well," he said when at last he could find his voice once more.

No one spoke for a long while, and Cass finished his portion of stew. "Thank you," he said to Greenlee and went to rinse his plate in the basin.

A low sound began to fill the room, sort of a moan or a keening, and Cass turned to find Quella, eyes closed, beginning to rock gently back and forth. The moan turned into a humming sound, and he realized it was a chant he'd heard as a child in Echoe. She seemed to be going into a trance. Neither man dared to interrupt whatever was happening, but the hair on Cass's neck rose.

Shortly, her breathing became rapid, and her eyelids fluttered although they remained closed. She spoke a few words, but her voice was so low Cass couldn't make out what she said.

Then, as if nothing unusual had transpired, she opened her eyes and spoke in a stronger voice.

"There is going to be a new way on this land," she said without any emotion attached to her statement. "This I have been told by the old fathers. No more Cherokee land. No more English land. The white man will prevail. The tribes will fade. Many will die before this happens."

A chill ran through Cass. "What do you mean, a new way?" he asked her.

"A third way. A new country."

Cass recalled the Regulators and their fight to gain some say in their government, but no one had talked about breaking away from the rule of the English king. It was unthinkable. "How, Quella? What is to happen?" He was almost afraid to hear her answer.

"Many wars, many battles. Many will die," she repeated, then added, "But you will not."

She grew quiet, and when she spoke again, her demeanor had returned to normal. She turned her clouded eyes on him.

"You are not of our people, Firehead, even though you know us well. You belong with your mother and white father. You must be loyal to them in this fight."

"But Onacona..." he started to protest, but Quella cut him short.

"Onacona was killed by an English bullet. If you wish to avenge his death and return to Cherokee balance, it is the English you must fight."

Cass knew Will Gordon hated the English because of what had happened in a battle long ago back in Scotland. His mother seemed more tolerant, but he knew she despised many of the English, especially the men. He suspected his blood father had been an Englishman who must have been cruel to her. Fiona had told him his father was dead. He had a sudden horrid thought: had his mother killed his father and run away?

Quella's vision quest had answered one of his questions—he was a white man, not an Indian, and he was to be loyal to his white family. But now other questions raged through his mind. About his father. About his mother. And about the fighting Quella had predicted. He raised his eyes to meet hers, to ask these questions.

But her eyes were closed now. She was slumped forward in her chair. Quella Longtree had lived long enough to deliver her message to Cass. And then she'd made her passing.

CHAPTER THREE

Hillsborough, North Carolina

Fiona and Will and their family grieved each in their own way after the departure of Aidan. Fiona missed her son terribly, but in a way, she was relieved he had left when he did.

Firehead was also a bit of a hothead, and the troubles between the English and the Regulators continued to get worse. She was certain he would have become involved in the battle at Alamance Creek where the British had killed several of their neighbors and captured and hanged six others.

Many who had survived had gathered under the direction of Colonel James Robertson and left the area, headed for the promised land of freedom, the Watauga Settlement. They were afraid of British retribution, and none was willing to sign a loyalty oath to the king.

"It's the only way out of this mess," one of them told Will. "Won't you come along?"

Will and Fiona discussed the possibility, but Fiona's Sight warned her against it. "Those people are die-hard Regulators and agitators," she told Will. "They'll bubble up trouble wherever they go." At the same time, she believed it was time for them to move on, just not to Watauga. She remembered the Golden Valley whispering her name and suggested moving to the Catawba River area. "Didn't you tell me your friend Sam Davidson went out there?"

"Yes, but...the problem is, we have no money to buy land, and a lot of his friends are speculators who've grabbed up the land grants and are selling the land, not re-granting it."

Fiona reached up and ran a finger down his nose and touched his lips. "Ah, husband, but we have some coin to our name," she said in Gaelic, the secret language they used when they wanted no one to understand what they said. Fiona shared that she had been squirreling away any hard currency that came their way, through her medicine work or his blacksmithing. It wasn't a lot, but it might be enough for a new beginning.

George and Emily Paterson were not hard to convince to join them. "We've traveled these hills together for many years," Will told George when he visited him after he and Fiona had determined to move to the Catawba Valley. "Come with us again."

And so later that year, after Will had arranged to secure some land from a man named McDowell, the two families, the Paterson's enlarged by the marriage of some of their children, set off again, heading west. Abe and Alicia refused Will's repeated offer of freedom and chose to join the caravan as perceived slaves.

* * *

Catawba Valley, August 1771

Fiona's back hurt from riding on the wagon for the many days it took them to journey from Hillsborough to the great open space that was the Catawba Valley. She hadn't told Will yet, but she suspected she was with child again. She also hadn't told Will why they hadn't had another child since Fergus was born. It was against many religious beliefs, but not her own. Fiona had used an ancient herbal formula for preventing conception. She already had four children, plus a settlement she served as a medicine woman. She hadn't wanted another child, until recently, after they'd decided to remove from Hillsborough. Maybe here, in the valley that had so strongly called to her, a new life would flourish.

Will had sent a message ahead of them to Sam Davidson, who met them at Quaker Meadows, homestead of some of the McDowells, who'd lived in the valley for several years.

Their own new landlord, a man with the colorful name of Hunting John McDowell, lived further to the west.

Margaret McDowell was a cordial hostess, and she seemed happy to have more settlers moving into the area. After the noontime dinner, she sat on the large porch, visiting with Fiona and the other women while the men inspected the horses that Joseph and his older son, Charles, fancied in racing. A younger son, also named Joseph, tagged along. Abe was assigned to care for the horses, and Alicia was instructed to join Margaret's servants in the kitchen. Fiona winced at the condescending treatment the McDowells showed to her African friends, but then, she knew that was the way of slave owners. It was just that she'd never considered the two as her slaves.

Talk on the porch turned to romance. "You won't be alone," Margaret assured Jeannette, who at age seventeen was anxious about not being able to meet eligible young men. "The Alexanders have moved here, and lots of McDowells have been here for some time. My own brothers and their families have farms around here as well."

She spoke of community gatherings, where other settlers helped one another build homes and barns, attended church services, and enjoyed picnics and dances. The picture she painted was an easy one for Fiona and Emily to embrace, for it was what they had been hoping for since coming to America those many years ago. Fiona noticed Margaret never once mentioned a threat of an Indian raid, and she wasn't going to bring it up. She hoped it wasn't mentioned because there had never been one.

When they prepared to continue their journey the next day, Fiona described to Sam Davidson the valley she remembered, not mentioning that she'd heard it whisper her name. Sam had offered to show them the way to Pleasant Gardens, home of Hunting John McDowell. "I think I know the place," he said. "We'll pass by there on the way."

When they reached the golden meadow, the pull of that open valley was even stronger than before, and Fiona insisted that the wagons stop by the riverside for a respite. The summer sun was warm, but it sparkled on the water, and Fiona and many of the others removed their shoes and dangled their feet in the cool water. "Is this the land we have purchased from Mr. McDowell?" she asked Davidson later as she handed him a piece of the fried chicken Margaret McDowell had packed for the journey.

"I don't know, ma'am. But I reckon he owns all the acres around here, so it's possible."

Fiona's hopes soared. She didn't know what it was about this land that called to her so strongly, only that she felt it down to the tip of her toes. This was to be her new home.

When they at last reached Pleasant Gardens, they found Hunting John to be far different from his brother Joseph. Where Joseph considered himself something of a country gentleman, John was obviously a backwoodsman turned landowner. Joseph had warned them of his rough nature, but Fiona found him delightful. He'd been a long hunter, from whence he gained his name, and like Sam Davidson and a few others, he had challenged the wilderness, and the English treaties, by stepping across boundaries and moving into forbidden territory.

"Had to settle down a bit when these two came along," he said, indicating his teenage children, Joseph and Rachel. He and his wife, Annie, lived in a simple log home, one built in two sections with a dog trot in between. Fiona wondered fleetingly if everyone around here had a son named Joseph. That could get confusing, she thought, slightly amused.

The families camped out alongside a tributary of the main river, a place called Buck Creek, a pleasant garden for sure. But Fiona was anxious to get on with the land purchase. It was time to begin their new life...again.

CHAPTER FOUR

Watauga Settlement, Autumn 1771

Many new settlers had come to the village since Cass had arrived, a number of them from around the Hillsborough area. They were former Regulators who were escaping English punishment for inciting violence in their quest for more governmental fairness. He learned that the movement had been defeated at the battle of Alamance in the spring of last year, when the governor's troops had easily routed the larger but disorganized band of dissenters. Some on both sides had been killed, and several Regulators were captured and hanged. Cass worried that Will and the Paterson men might have been among them, but after asking around, no one had heard their names among the casualties, so it seemed they had survived the fray.

After the Alamance defeat, Colonel Robertson had brought sixteen Regulator families across the mountains. Those who had moved to Watauga spoke words that would be treasonous should they be caught, words like "independence" and "freedom." There was a movement, they said, in Philadelphia and Boston, toward creating a new country, America, and booting the British out.

There will be a new way. A third way. A new country.

Quella's prophecy rang in Cass's ears. Was this possible?

He and Greenlee had buried Quella the morning after her death and performed a Cherokee ritual over her grave. The old trader had told him that his own Cherokee wife had died of the smallpox, and that although Quella had come to tend her, she had been unable to save her.

After that, Quella herself had grown frail and needed help, so he'd ended up sharing her cabin and caring for her between trading trips.

After they buried Quella, Greenlee had accompanied Cass into the Watauga Settlement and introduced him around. He'd remained there over the summer months, establishing new contacts for his business, and in truth, trying to figure which way the wind blew as pertained to the Indians, the British, and these brash settlers.

Then it was time for him to go. "I'm headed back toward Salisbury and points south," Greenlee told Cass as he climbed onto his wagon. "If I see Will Gordon, I will tell him we met up."

"Thank you for your kindness, sir," Cass said. "Please let my ma know I'm all right."

* * *

Cass found the men and women who had come to Watauga, not just the Regulators but many from Virginia as well, to be of strong will with a determination not to live by English law.

They defied a British decree that outlawed white settlement west of the mountains and their consequent demand for all settlers to return to legal territory. They'd formed the Watauga Association to negotiate their own treaty directly with the Cherokee, and they were devising a set of their own rules by which to govern what they considered to be an independent state.

Colonel Robertson proposed a novel solution: "The English say we're not supposed to settle on these lands, which the Cherokee claim is theirs. But what if we pay the Indians to use it? What if we were to lease it?"

Cass found this a reasonable alternative to having all these people leave everything they'd built—their homes and fields and crops. Certainly, a better option than going to war with the Cherokee, as some had proposed, to win the land through bloodshed. Perhaps this was a way the whites and reds might peacefully live together.

The meetings where the details of this new government were being hammered out were lively affairs. Among those joining the discussions were a couple of veteran frontiersmen, John Sevier and Isaac Shelby, who were outspoken on the need to shake off English restrictions on westward expansion. Another woodsman he met there was the famous scout and long hunter, Daniel Boone, who spoke up in favor of staying the course at Watauga. "Now's the time to keep the country," he told them. "For if we give it up now, it will ever be the same."

Cass thought he recalled Will having mentioned that the Boone family had once been his neighbors when he'd lived on the Yadkin, and at the close of the meeting, he drew up his courage to ask Boone if he was of that family. Daniel grinned broadly and said he remembered the Gordon and McKinney families well.

"Good folk, those. Sad what happened to their family. After that massacre, I sent Rebecca and our children back to Virginia during those times."

Cass also met a trader, who was a gunsmith and a blacksmith as well, named Jacob Brown who lived over on the Nolichucky River but who had temporarily come back to Watauga.

After one of these meetings, the two repaired to a local tavern for a brew. Brown said he needed to catch up on these recent events, as he had been gone on a hunting trip on the Toe River with an old friend, Hunting John McDowell.

Cass had heard of McDowell—he was almost as well known a long hunter as Daniel Boone—and he was eager to learn more about him.

"McDowell's a shrewd businessman, despite his rough looks. Owns a lot of land in the Catawba Valley and has his eye on more along the Toe River," Brown told him. "I think he might even be casting an eye beyond the Tanase after hearing the tales of Boone and his party exploring over in Kaintuck."

"The Cherokee will never stand for it," Cass said, recalling from his childhood the ferocious warriors who'd come to Echoe to raise a war party from time to time to attack isolated settlements that had encroached on Cherokee land.

Brown laughed. "You know what they say. Money talks. I think these boys here in Watauga might be onto something in working it out to lease their land," he told Cass. "See no reason I can't do the same with my land. I'd have to do it separate because it's outside of the Watauga settlement. In the meantime, I'm going back to the Nolichucky."

Cass learned that Brown had settled on the north side of the Nolichucky River with two other families. He had a small trading post through which he supplied the Cherokees with European goods. "Got a good relationship with them," Brown said. "They like the guns I make for them, and the black powder and shot I sell them. I'll wait and see how this works out for Watauga and make my own agreement with them then."

Cass was energized by this talk of greater freedom from English law, and he saw no harm to the Cherokee people if they got paid for letting the settlers use their land. They were going to use it anyway, it would seem. It was now autumn in the high country, and another cold winter in the mountains had lost its appeal. He made Brown a proposition.

"I speak Cherokee," Cass told him. "I'm a fair hand at blacksmithing too. Might you need an assistant?"

Brown didn't turn him down outright, but rather studied him over his glass. "How come you speak Cherokee? You're a gingerhead."

At that Cass laughed. "Actually, I was born in a Cherokee town, Echoe, but my mother was Irish. When I came out of her with a mop of red hair, my Cherokee grandmother called me Firehead." He hoped Brown wouldn't pursue his questioning because Cass couldn't answer much else about his beginnings, and he was glad when his new friend changed the subject.

"So, you want to come with me," Brown stated. "You say you were born in Echoe, but I heard you came from back east. Ever lived out in the woods? Any good with a gun?"

Cass bristled at the insinuation that he was a green woodsman. "I was raised by Indians until I was eight. Learned a lot of their ways before going back to white civilization. I left Hillsborough on my own more than a year ago. Hunted and trapped my way up here. Guess you could say I'm good in the woods and good with a gun. But if you don't need me..." Cass got up and started to leave before his temper flared.

"Now, now, don't go getting' all riled up," Brown said. "Here, have another ale. This one's on me."

CHAPTER FIVE

Watauga Settlement, Spring 1772

James Robertson and John Bean, the emissaries who were chosen to go to Chota to treat with the Cherokees for the lease of the Watauga lands, returned having successfully presented their proposal that was accompanied by many gifts. The details of the arrangement were to be finalized upon the visit of Attakulakula, the old and respected peace chief of the Cherokee, who would arrive in Watauga soon. Cass and Jacob attended the meeting where the two reported on their visit.

"It's clear to us that the Cherokees are deeply divided over this," Robertson told them. "We're fortunate that the elders prevailed. The young warriors, egged on by one named Dragging Canoe, who is Attakulakula's son, want no peace with us. They've been betrayed by the English many times, as treaties have frequently been made only to be broken, and they trust no white man."

This wasn't anything new to Cass. He'd been hearing such things since he was a boy in Echoe, and later from Will and others who'd faced the natives' fierce opposition by way of Indian attacks.

A short time later, after the old chief and the Wataugans had agreed to some "Articles of Friendship," a lease agreement was executed. The Cherokee received upward of five thousand Colonial pounds in merchandise and trade goods, muskets, and household items. The Wataugans received the use of all the country along the Watauga River.

Jacob Brown then went to work. "If they can do it, so can I," he told Cass eagerly shortly thereafter. "My only problem is a certain lack of funding. But I have an idea. I want you to deliver a letter to my old friend Hunting John."

That night, by the light of a flickering candle, the two drafted a letter in which Jacob explained his proposition to lease from the Cherokee the large tracts of land he already occupied, just as the Wataugans had done. He asked for money and trade goods from McDowell to help fund the enterprise, promising in return that he would sign over two large tracts of the leased land to the old longhunter. Not wanting to hold his negotiations so close to the Watauga settlement, in case there were any reprisals from those young Indians who had been against the Watauga arrangement, he requested that the transaction take place on McDowell's land at Pleasant Gardens.

"Isn't that quite a distance from here?" Cass asked, taking the letter and preparing to leave at daylight. "Will the Indians travel that far to treat with you?"

Jacob winked at him. "Like I said, boy, money talks. When I hear back from John, I will know how much I can offer. Them Indians have traveled longer distances than that in their dealings with the English. We shall see." He thought for a moment, then added, "Also, by having the Indians come to his land, John will see this is a legitimate negotiation, not some scheme to just take his money."

* * *

Cass left before dawn, following a roughly drawn map that would take him over the mountains and down into the Catawba Valley and Hunting John's place, Pleasant Gardens. He pondered Jacob's last comment about this not being a scheme to cheat Hunting John. Had Jacob cheated him in the past? He wondered what kind of reception awaited him in the valley below.

He was also annoyed at the trader's condescending manner in sending him on this mission, although he didn't mind getting back into the isolation of the forest.

The trail down the mountain was an old Indian trading path, and he had no trouble following it along the ridgelines. But his horse stumbled and almost fell as they embarked on the steep descent from the mountain top, so Cass dismounted and walked alongside the animal until they came to lower ground. He saw no one along the way, of red skin or white.

When he reached a creek at the foot of the steep mountain, he paused and looked over the vast expanse of open land that lay before him. It was indeed pleasant to the eye, and he could understand why so many settlers wanted to move here. From what he'd heard, this valley was legally open for settlement, although the Indians thought otherwise. The boundary, he had been told, was those high mountains he'd just crossed.

Moving on, he soon came upon what was marked on the map as the Catawba River, which was wider than the creek he'd passed earlier. But as he followed it upstream, it narrowed and became shallower, and eventually he managed to cross it. He was just coming out of the water when he heard a shout, and he reined in his horse sharply. He searched the woods for an attacker, but no one was there.

He heard more shouts, some even sounding like whoops, and then cheering. He cautiously followed the ruckus and came upon a clearing where a small crowd was gathered around two men who were mounted on horses. He took cover in the thick shade of the trees that lined the clearing and watched, curious as to what was going on. The men dismounted and led the horses away, while three others approached on mounts of their own. The crowd backed away, and the riders lined up abreast. A shrill whistle sounded, and the men spurred their horses. It was a race! A horse race right here in the mountains!

Cass had heard of the wealthy planters back east holding such races, but he'd never seen one. And he had never thought the backwoods people would have either the quality of horses or the time for such genteel entertainment. With a grin, he nudged his horse out of the shadows and rode at a canter toward the gathering. The second race had finished, and the riders were returning to the crowd before anyone spotted him. When they did, the menfolk stepped in front of the women and children, guns at their sides but not raised. Cass drew his horse to a halt and raised his hand in greeting.

"Hallo! I've come from over the mountains with a message for Mr. Hunting John McDowell. Has anyone here heard of him?"

At this, a titter of laughter ripped through the group. A tall man stepped forward. "I am he," he said. "And you would be...?"

"Name's Cass. Cass Gordon. Come to bring you a message from a friend, Jacob Brown."

Cass wasn't sure, but he thought he saw McDowell roll his eyes. "Brown, huh? What does he want now?" he muttered, just loud enough that Cass caught his words. Then McDowell motioned to him. "Get on down now. Come and eat. We're just havin' us a big party."

Cass swung down from the mare, and as he turned, he saw a young woman running toward him. "Aidan!" she called. "Aidan! Is that you?"

And Jeannette Gordon hurled herself into his arms.

Cass scarcely had time to comprehend who she was when others broke from the crowd and came running. Will, Maura, and Fergus were headed his way at a sprint, followed by the Paterson men, all waving and shouting in greeting. And then he saw his mother following more slowly, a babe in her arms. Tears sprang to his eyes. He'd been away almost two years, and in that time, he hadn't considered what might be happening with his family. He just assumed they were still in Hillsborough. He'd promised himself one day he would return for a visit, but he never had.

Jeannette continued to cling to him, sobbing with joy, but the others made way for Fiona, her red hair gleaming in the sun. She stared at him for a long moment, obviously in as much disbelief as he was. "Aidan," she managed at last. "You're alive!"

He drew his mother into his arms. He was taller than she by almost a head, and he hid his tears in the fullness of her hair. "Yes, Ma. I'm alive. And so are you." And they both started to laugh when the baby protested to being squeezed between them. "I see someone else is alive too," Cass said, peering into the brilliant green eyes that stared back at him. "Who have we here?"

"This is your sister, Kate," Fiona said, and handed the baby to him. He saw she had a red fuzz on her head, and those green eyes! How startling they were! He fell in love with her instantly. Cradling her in his arms, he suddenly realized how much he had missed his family.

How much they loved him, how hard it must have been on them when he left and not knowing his fate all this time.

He handed the baby back to Fiona, aware that Jeannette was still attached to his arm. He turned and started to chide her and make her let go, but the young woman he saw wasn't the girl he'd grown up with, the girl who became his sister when her father adopted him. This girl had ripened into a woman whose pretty face was framed by playful golden curls. "Jeannette?"

"Of course, silly," she replied. "Oh, Aidan, I'm so glad you are safe and back home."

Her words sobered him. Back home. Where was home? How did his family come to be out here? And, he knew, this wasn't his home. His home lay in those high mountains.

CHAPTER SIX

Fiona had scarcely dared to breathe when she saw the man astride the gray horse approaching them. Even from a distance, she'd known it was Aidan. There was no mistaking the Firehead when he'd removed his hat. She had sorely missed him and often fretted over his well being, but in her heart, she had never felt he was in harm's way. Still, seeing him here was a shock even her Sight hadn't prepared her for.

As she'd embraced her son, she'd felt his strength, smelled his man scent, and knew he was a boy no longer. After he managed to extricate himself from Jeannette, Fiona looked him in the eyes. "Have you come home?" she asked, and immediately saw his confusion. "Oh, of course. You wouldn't know where home is anymore, now would you?" She wasn't scolding, rather laughing at herself to think he had any idea they had moved away from Hillsborough.

"No, Ma. Where is your home now?"

She didn't miss the nuance in his answer. Your home. Not his home, and she knew they wouldn't hold him here for long.

As the families strolled together toward a log cabin, she tried to compress all that had happened with them in the past two years into a few minutes but wasn't finished when they reached the shade trees in front of the dwelling. "There's more. Much more. We must catch up fully later. But now our host beckons."

John McDowell stood on his front porch and rang a bell. "Annie and I invited you here to celebrate the end of a good summer," he said, raising a glass. "There has been no Indian trouble, crops have been plentiful, and we have new neighbors moving steadily into our valley." Which suited McDowell fine, Fiona thought wryly, since he was the one profiting from selling them their land.

"Today we have even more reason to celebrate," McDowell continued. "The return of Aidan Gordon, Will and Fiona's oldest boy. Will says he's a longhunter like myself, been out there a couple of years. Welcome to the Catawba Valley, son!" At that he invited them all to enjoy the feast he and Annie and their children had prepared for the festivities. They had killed some of their hogs and roasted them slowly over an open fire. There was corn fresh from the field, and tomatoes and peaches, melons slashed open to reveal their sweet redness. Freshly baked bread and blackberry pie.

"You must be famished," she said to Aidan, and balancing Kate, her youngest, in one arm, she took Aidan, her oldest, by the hand and led him to the groaning picnic table. She noticed she didn't have to ask him twice. She also noticed that Jeannette seemed unable to keep her eyes off him.

Will came up behind her. "What a wonderful surprise," he said, and kissed her cheek. "A great day it is indeed."

"You are a fine man, Will Gordon," she took his work-roughened hand and kissed it. "Seems you've forgiven him for his ill-treatment of you as he left."

He laughed and took his new little girl in his arms. "Ah, tosh, that was nothing but a young man trying to find himself." He studied Aidan, who was now surrounded by the younger folks in the crowd who were obviously eager to hear the tales of his adventures in the wilderness.

"Seems he's done that all right. But I'm curious about how he came to be here, and what's in that message he says he bears."

Shortly, she saw Hunting John beckon Aidan away from the others, and the two retreated into one of the two connected cabins. "I suspect Mr. McDowell wonders the same. Hopefully we will learn something soon."

That night, by the light of their campfire, Aidan related much of what had transpired since he'd left them in Hillsborough. Fiona listened with growing interest as he told them about the fiercely independent people in the Watauga settlement who seemed unafraid to take on either the Indians or the English, and in fact were creating a separate government. Aidan had told them about the Wataugans' bold move to lease land from the Cherokee, which brought him to why he'd come to McDowell's plantation. "Jacob is hoping to lease his lands, which lie outside the Watauga settlement, in a similar manner."

"How does this Jacob Brown know John McDowell?" Fiona asked.

Aidan explained that Brown and a small party of refugees from South Carolina had passed through here on their way into the mountains, and he'd struck up a friendship with Hunting John, both being avid hunters. "They've had several hunting expeditions together since then, Jacob told me. Apparently, he borrowed a bit of money from McDowell as he left the last time, which he used to pay a squatter to leave the property on the Nolichucky that he wanted. Hunting John told me he'd never paid it back, and now he's asking for more."

"Why would McDowell want to lend him more?" Will frowned.

Aidan gave a low laugh. "Jacob has a saying. 'Money talks.' He needs money and trade goods from Hunting John to secure these leases, and he knows John is hungry for land beyond those mountains. So he's offered him two large tracts of the land he proposes to lease from the Cherokee in repayment."

"Is John going to give him the money?" Fiona said, skeptical of the whole idea.

Aidan hesitated, then replied with a shake of his head, "I don't know. There's more to it than the money. Jacob doesn't want to negotiate with the Cherokee up there on the mountains because the Watauga negotiations weren't exactly easy or friendly. The tribal elders were in favor, but the young warriors almost threatened war. Jacob thinks doing similar negotiations near Watauga might be dangerous if the younger warriors should get wind of it and try to prevent yet another lease."

"So, what is he asking in addition to the funding?" Will pressed.

Aidan looked out into the darkness. "That the Indians be invited here for the signing."

"Here!" Fiona cried, appalled to think of any Indians being invited into lands where so many had died at their hands. "Why, isn't that a fair distance for them to come?"

"He thinks they'll come if enough money and trade goods are offered, and he also thinks this is a way to prove to John this isn't just a scheme to abscond with more money. If the Indians come to Pleasant Gardens, Mr. McDowell can see the transaction for himself."

Will couldn't stifle his "humph," and Fiona had to agree. Aidan seemed to trust this Jacob Brown, but she sensed John McDowell would never acquire a single acre from this deal.

She held her tongue, however. It was none of her business, as long as Aidan wasn't somehow caught in the middle and thought to be a cheat.

Later, after all were bedded down near the fire for the night, Fiona saw Aidan leave the circle of light cast by the dying fire. She rose and followed him into the darkness and cleared her throat before she got too close, to let him know she was there.

He didn't turn, but said, "Hello, Ma. I thought you'd come." She reached his side, and he took her hand. "There's more I need to tell you, but not in the company of others."

They strolled together beneath the stars that in this moonless night illuminated the open field with twinkling glory. On the meadow before them, fireflies blinked as if in answer. Fiona didn't speak but waited for Aidan to begin.

"I saw Quella," he said at last. "She was in a cabin in the high mountains. A man named Hiram Greenlee was with her. He was a trader. I think he knew Pa Will." Aidan was silent for a long while. Then he said, "Quella told me she delivered Jeannette when she was born."

"I believe that to be true. Will told me about it. He said she came the very night his wife went into labor. He didn't know how she knew to come just at that moment."

"Isn't is queer, Ma, how she seemed to just know things?"

Fiona smiled inwardly. Aidan had no idea about the Indian spirit visions of his grandmother and Quella, or in fact, about Fiona's own ability to read the unseen. "What did Quella say to you?"

"She said..." Aidan broke off here, and Fiona knew whatever was coming was difficult for him. "She said she talked with Onacona in the spirit world. I think I saw her do it that night I was with her. She said... he told her that I must stay with my white people. That as much as I felt close to the Indian ways, they aren't my natural ways."

In a way, Fiona felt a great relief at this, but at the same time, she wasn't sure how Aidan felt about it. So, she asked him.

"I am white," he said simply. "As far as my skin goes anyway. But Ma, I can't abide many of the white man's ways. I felt I would choke if I stayed in Hillsborough any longer. I don't belong in towns, or on a farm. The forests and mountains are my home now."

"This I know," she replied. "It is how you must be." But the night seemed to get a little darker.

"There's one more thing, Ma," her son said. "In the mountains, I found my true self. I'm a different person now, and, well, I am no longer Aidan. They call me Cass."

CHAPTER SEVEN

On the Nolichucky River, 1772

Cass returned with the news that John McDowell would welcome a party of Cherokee chiefs to his plantation and would host them for the duration of the negotiations, providing they not stay for an extended period, and that there would be no violence against his family or any of the white settlers. Jacob Brown wasted no time in contacting Attakulakula, using some of his Cherokee customers to deliver the invitation, along with the lucrative offer he was making with John McDowell's funding.

In less than a fortnight, a contingent of Cherokees from Chota arrived at Brown's Trading Post. Cass was in awe at meeting Attakulakula, the Peace Chief, and Oconostata, the War Chief, two of the most honored and respected chiefs in the tribe, men he had heard about since childhood. In fact, his Ma had told him Attakulakula had been through Echoe more than once, but he'd been too young to remember.

Both were old men now, but somehow still regal in demeanor. Attakulakula wore a bright red cape with gold striping over blue breeches and an elegant white shirt. Cass had heard this man had been to England and met the king. Oconostata was in similar dress, and both wore many beads, a heavy metal gorget at the neck, and fanciful silver ornaments in their ears. In looks as well as mannerisms, they commanded an impressive presence.

Brown welcomed them heartily and produced some small gifts. "We are honored that you have come," he told the chiefs. "But I must ask, what of Dragging Canoe? Does he know of your mission?"

The two glanced at one another, then Oconostata replied. "He was not in the village when we left." Cass took that as a no, and he was relieved.

Before proceeding down the mountains, they and others who had come along with them met with Brown under a large oak on his property, where the two parties agreed upon loosely written "Articles of

Friendship" similar to those of the Watauga lease. No money or goods changed hands at this point, but Brown had a map that clearly showed the lands which he was proposing to lease, insisting that the chiefs understand what he was asking.

Although Brown spoke some Cherokee, he used Cass as his translator. "Make sure they understand that we are not asking to own the land, only to use it, just as the Wataugans are."

Then he added under his breath, "They should know by now that once the whites are on the land, they aren't going to leave—ever, lease or no lease."

Cass was doubtful that this, or the Watauga lease, was legal, but he dutifully translated Brown's words, made sure the Indians understood the arrangement, and that the hand-drawn map depicted what they were willing to sign over to Brown. Jacob signed his name, and the Indians made their mark, and the next day the entourage moved toward the Catawba Valley.

Before they arrived at Pleasant Gardens, Cass went ahead to alert John McDowell and his family of their approaching visitors. "That didn't take as long as I thought," the wizened longhunter said with a grin. "Jacob must want to strike while the deal-making is hot." He called to Annie and rounded up his grown children, Joseph and Rachel. He sent them to bring others in the valley to lend a hand in preparing for the Indians, including his nephews from Quaker Meadows and the Davidsons and Alexanders from further up the valley. "I could use those Paterson fellas from over your Ma's way, and Will and his man slave, too, if they can be spared. Would you ride and fetch them for me?" he asked Cass.

He directed Cass toward Will's land purchase and sent him on his way. Cass had earlier taken a little offense at being ordered to be an errand boy for Jacob Brown, but McDowell had asked, not ordered. And besides, Cass was elated to be able to visit his family's new homestead.

It was twilight when he approached the small log cabin not far from a creek that was a tributary of the Catawba. Jeannette was in the yard chopping wood with as much vigor as if she were a man, and Fergus, now eight, was carrying the firewood back to the cabin. From inside, Cass heard a baby's wail. He rode slowly into the clearing, wondering how Will was faring as a farmer with only the women, the young African Abe, and a small boy to help him work the land.

He felt a twinge of guilt. Maybe he should stay here, at least until Fergus was old enough to shoulder some of the burden.

But he knew in his heart he didn't belong here. Maybe the Paterson boys were helping Will out. Tomorrow he'd ride on over to their place, which he understood to be further downstream on the Catawba where George was once again running a grist mill. Tonight, though, he wanted only to be here, to see his family in their own home and know they were safe.

Jeannette spotted him first and shouted, "Ma, come quick! It's Aidan again!" This time she didn't rush to him but set down the hatchet and demurely wiped her hands on her apron.

Maura appeared at the front door, grinning but shy as she'd always been. Seeing her tugged at his heart, for he remembered how fearful and yet how brave she'd been as a little girl running away from Indian country. That had been more than ten years ago, and now she was almost full grown. Her Cherokee heritage was clear in her dark hair and eyes, high cheekbones and slanted nose. In some ways, she reminded him of Quella.

"Son!" Fiona cried, running out of the cabin as he dismounted. "You keep surprising us!"

"Well, Ma, I can leave..." he teased, but he picked her up by her waist and spun her around. She, too, was no longer young, but handsome as ever.

"Don't you fool with me, boy," she chided with a girlish giggle. "Come on inside. I'm just about done fixing supper. Will should be home any time now. He's been over at the mill with some of our corn."

* * *

Later that night, Cass sat with Will on a wooden bench on the small porch. "Looks like things are going well here," he said, wanting to learn if that indeed was true.

"Well enough, I suppose," Will replied. "The womenfolk seem contented, and we haven't seen any sign of Indians, although we've heard they still roam these parts."

Cass knew what had happened to Will's family back on the Yadkin, and he had to believe the older man lived with the worry that it could happen here. He wished he could reassure him, but he knew that all white settlers on the western frontiers of the colonies were at risk. Dragging Canoe had a strong following of young warriors, and Cass had no way of knowing if any of the older chiefs could restrain him for long.

"John asked me to fetch men from around here to help when the Indian treaty party arrives, which will likely be soon, if they aren't there already. But I think it would be a good idea for you to stay here with Ma and the children. I'll see if Jake and his brothers can be spared. George shouldn't come either. Even though you haven't seen any Indians doesn't mean that they won't come again. Somebody needs to stay on the homesteads just in case."

Out of the corner of his eye, he saw Will lean his head back against the rough logs of the cabin and close his eyes. "I suppose you're right," he said at last. "I have no wish to encounter any Indian, friend or foe." He paused again, then added, "You don't suppose this is some kind of ruse to get all the settlers over there in one place to attack them?"

That had never occurred to Cass, but he couldn't dismiss it as a possibility. "It could be, I suppose, but with Attakulakula leading them, I think it's unlikely. He is a firm friend of the English, and even though it's said he is against further westward settlement by white folk, he is also against unnecessary bloodshed. It's his son, Dragging Canoe, to be worried about, and we think he is unaware of this meeting."

"When you mentioned this at supper, Fiona remarked that Annie and Rachel would need help in preparing the food. You know your Ma is not one to be told what to do, and I think she's set her cap on going. So, we will all go. If Indians come here, the worst that can happen is they'll burn our home and destroy our crops. But then," he added with a sad note, "I helped do that in one of their villages once."

Cass heard the sorrow in his last words, but he didn't know what to say, so he remained quiet. The chorus of cicadas sang loudly from the trees, and the wind whispered through the leaves. A peaceful moment, he thought. Enjoy it now. Respect it, for who knows what tomorrow will bring.

CHAPTER EIGHT

Pleasant Gardens, North Carolina, Spring 1772

The family arrived at the McDowell place late the following afternoon. They had ridden their horses and left Alicia and Abe to bring up the wagon behind them with what food they could spare. If Cass was wrong and the Indians planned a surprise attack, they would have more chance of escape on horseback. But they felt compelled to bring what supplies they could in the wagon—corn meal ground at George's mill, the last of their corn harvest, and turnips and potatoes recently dug and ready to be stored for their winter food supply.

Fiona wondered as they rode how Will felt about the upcoming encounter with the Indians. He'd told her he'd resolved his need to revenge the deaths of his wife and her parents, but she wasn't sure that fire was completely out. Within his quiet depths, his gentle nature, she believed anger still smoldered. What would it take, she wondered, to fan those flames back to life? And when would that happen?

When they approached Pleasant Gardens from along the Catawba River, Fiona was alarmed to see a large encampment of Cherokee on the opposite side of the river, maybe over fifty assembled there. Had Hunting John counted on such a large contingent to feed and house for this event?

Cass halted the small group he'd assembled to assist McDowell in this crazy endeavor—the Paterson boys and others from neighboring farms. He, too, was surprised by their numbers. "Weren't that many with us up on the Nolichucky," he said, frowning as he urged his horse forward to greet the Indians.

As Fiona watched, she could tell he had a way with these people. He spoke their language, understood their ways. He was, she understood clearly, still part Cherokee. She glanced over at Maura, but her daughter's face was unreadable. Inscrutable as most Indians were at times. Still, as Maura stared unblinking at the natives, Fiona perceived an air of longing about her. She, too, was still part Cherokee.

When Cass returned, he directed them toward McDowell's cabin. Annie came running to greet them, reaching up for Kate while her son Joseph helped Fiona from her saddle. "Thank God you've come!" she cried. "I had no idea what we were in for!"

Fiona saw open cooking fires set up in the clearing, and a few men tended the roasting meat. "How many Indians are there?" she asked, taking Kate back into her arms.

"John estimates around fifty or sixty. It's going to clean us out of our stores!"

Fiona heard the panic in her voice. "Where's that man, that Jacob Brown?" she asked, wanting to take a switch to him for bringing such a burden to these people.

"He's with John right now. Man talk," Annie almost spat. "Don't know why John wants that land over the mountains. We've our hands full right here on the Catawba."

Fiona, Jeannette, and Maura followed Annie to where she'd set up an outdoor kitchen of sorts. Immediately they began preparing what they could in advance of the need to feed and maintain good will with the Indians. They were far outnumbered, and Fiona knew from experience that the Indian temperament could change with the wind. If something didn't please them, they could turn on their hosts in a heartbeat.

Jacob Brown and Hunting John McDowell emerged from the cabin and came over to where the women were hard at work. "Ladies, you are doing a wonderful service for us tonight," John said, kissing his wife.

"I just hope they eat and go away," Annie hissed, brushing him away.

He laughed. "Now Annie, you know that ain't going to happen. They're here for a party. For all the food and drink they can get before settling down to business."

"Dear God!" Annie muttered.

* * *

As John predicted, the Indians remained at Pleasant Gardens for the better part of two weeks. When they finally departed, it was as if locusts had stripped the place of its food and drink. But John McDowell got what he wanted, the promise of two large tracts of what Jacob was now calling the Brown Purchase. And Jacob got what he wanted, a signed document, leasing him the land. The Cherokee got what they wanted as well, money, guns and ammunition, livestock, corn, trade goods and trinkets. Fiona thought it was a hefty price for nothing more than a promise from Jacob Brown.

Cass didn't accompany the Indians back over the mountains right away. He stayed that night with his family and the rest of the settlers who had pitched in to help McDowell. It was a somber group that sat around a fire that evening. No one knew quite what to say, or what to think about the event.

Fiona and Will sat across the fire circle from Cass, and she saw Jeannette take a seat next to her stepbrother on one of the large logs that they'd laid in a circle around the fire pit. A seat a little too close to him, she thought. She saw Cass move to the side to give his sister more room, but Jeannette scooted next to him again and whispered something in his ear. He frowned, and a few moments later, he replied, shaking his head. Jeannette covered her face with her hands, then stood up and rushed away from him, into the shadows of the night. Fiona frowned. What was that all about?

The following morning, everyone moved quickly to set things to right for the McDowells, then headed back to their farms, hopeful they would find them untouched by Indians or outlaws. Cass accompanied them back to the Gordon farmstead. Jeannette hung back, asking if she could go with Alicia in the wagon, and gave Abe her horse to ride. Whatever Cass had said to her last night must have hurt her deeply, Fiona thought.

That night, Cass and Will again sat together on the porch while Fiona and the older children put the younger ones to bed. Jeannette excused herself as well and climbed into the loft where she slept. Fiona wasn't sure, but she thought she heard soft sobs moments later.

Fiona and Maura stepped out onto the porch with the men. Wind had begun to whip the trees, and a storm was in the air. Suddenly Maura said, "What did you say to Jeannette last night that's got her so upset?"

"Maura! That is none of your business!" Fiona scolded.

"It's all right, Ma," Aidan said.

She must stop thinking of him as Aidan. He wanted to be Cass. It could be worse. He might have chosen an Indian name. What if he'd decided to be called Firehead?

"She's crying," Maura said. "You made her cry. Why?"

"She...well, she wanted something from me I can't give her," he said after a long hesitation. "I told her to forget it."

"What?" Maura was insistent. "What could you have that she'd want?"

"Me."

An astonished silence fell among them. Then Maura said, "I don't understand."

"She said she wanted me to be her fella," Cass said awkwardly. "She's a pretty girl and all, but, well, she's my sister. I can't..."

Will spoke then. "I married a girl that I was raised up with as a sister," he said. "Not blood kin, but still a part of her family. But what we had between us became more of a bond than between brother and sister. It was all right in the eyes of God and our family. But Aidan, I mean Cass, it was something special we felt between us. It's not likely that you have those feelings for Jeannette, especially after having been gone for a long time."

Cass stood and went to the edge of the porch. "It's not just Jeannette. I don't think I'd be much good to any woman," he told them. "I can't seem to stay in one place very long. I have to be on the move, to live free, and not be beholden to anyone."

The Great Spirit put rocks in my moccasins. Quella would have understood his restless ways, Fiona thought.

"We know you would never do anything to hurt Jeannette," she told Cass. "It was a romantic notion on her part."

"I didn't encourage her, Ma, I promise."

"We know that. This isn't your fault. She'll be over it tomorrow, likely."

"Doubt it," Maura said. "All she wants is to find a man and get married."

Come morning, Cass was gone.

***

Salisbury, North Carolina, May 1773

Will stood erect beside the bride, his only child of the few years he'd had with Margaret. Jeannette looked lovely this morning, dressed in white linen with flowers in her hair. In a few moments, she would wed Philemon Means, a traveling preacher man who'd started making his rounds in the Catawba Valley shortly after the Jacob Brown affair last fall.

Services were held mostly in barns or if the weather permitted, under the shade of the many large trees that had not been cleared for cultivation. One such service had been held at their farm, and afterward, Fiona had invited the young preacher to stay for dinner. After that, Philemon had found frequent excuses to call between stops in his pastoral duties, and it soon became apparent to both Fiona and Will that he had more on his mind than saving their souls.

It had been hard on Fiona to learn that Jeannette, who was like her own daughter, planned to move to Salisbury after they were wed, where Philemon had his main congregation. But Will could tell she was happy that at last Jeannette had found the husband she had longed for. He hoped the preacher would be the good husband he wanted for his daughter.

Since Philemon was the minister in this church, he'd called upon a magistrate with the legal authority to perform marriages, to preside. After Will had responded to the question, "Who giveth this woman in marriage?" he took his seat on the front row and entwined his fingers with Fiona's. She squeezed his hand, and both looked straight forward, each not wanting to see the tears that welled in the other's eyes.

After the ceremony, the entire congregation emerged into a bright spring day. Mary and Jake hugged the bride and congratulated the groom, then Mary dashed off with her daughters, now in their teens, to oversee the laying out of the wedding feast. Many of their neighbors from the Catawba had made the journey, and Will suspected the women were especially in need of a respite from the drudge of farm duties. They all seemed in high spirits, talking and laughing, taking turns congratulating the couple. Philemon had arranged with local women to provision the feast, and the table groaned beneath the weight of roasted turkey, ham, potatoes cooked in milk and onions, fresh corn and other vegetables, cornbread and wheat bread hot out of the oven, and numerous fruit pies. It seemed to Will a sign that this man would take good care of Jeannette.

After the feast, he brought out a fiddle and handed it to Fiona. "Won't the mother of the bride give us a tune?" he asked, taking up his own fiddle to back her up.

"Would it be proper?" Fiona asked, but Will saw her fingers already playing with the strings. Playing music together had been an integral part of their lives ever since Will had given his father-in-law's fiddle to her, and both had become quite accomplished.

Fiona chose a lively jig to start the dancing, and as Will knew she would, Jeannette began to tap her toes. In her love for dancing, she was just like her mother. He'd never known Jeannette to sit still once the music started and dancing commenced. Her wedding day was no different. She took her husband by the hand and led him to a flat area on the grounds in front of the church and proceeded to encourage him to dance with her.

Philemon Means was not a dancer, that much was obvious to Will. But even more, he stood there frowning, and Will had the premonition that maybe this was one of those preachers who didn't believe in such frivolities. Jeannette was distressed, but just gave it up and laughed her way back into the crowd as if her new husband's hesitation was nothing. Then Will saw Jake come to Jeannette's rescue by asking her to dance and encouraging the others to join in the merriment. As Will and Fiona moved on to a new tune, he noticed the groom standing behind the crowd, a scowl on his face, and his heart was saddened. Philemon Means might be an upright man and a good preacher, but he suddenly doubted Jeannette's choice of a husband. Could she, so light of spirit, find happiness with such a dour man?

Chapter Nine

Brown's Purchase, Autumn 1774

A group of Cherokees rode into the clearing at Brown's Trading Post, and Cass could smell trouble. These were not their usual customers, and their faces were painted with black streaks. He reached for his rifle and stepped to the front door of the cabin.

"*Siyo!*" he said in Cherokee greeting. One of the warriors cocked his head and looked closely at him from behind his war paint.

"Firehead?"

Cass squinted to try to see who this was calling him by his boyhood name. Something about him seemed familiar. "*Vv,*" he replied, "yes."

The man said something to the others in his party that Cass couldn't quite make out, then he dismounted and came over to him. "Do you remember me?" he asked in Cherokee. Seeing him close up, Cass did remember.

"Dustu?"

At this the young warrior broke out into a wide grin and said in Cherokee, "It was you who broke my nose when I teased you about your red hair."

Cass remembered the incident clearly. After the fistfight that had ensued, during which he'd broken the boy's nose, the two had become fast friends. The last time he'd seen Dustu was the day they'd left Echoe for good.

He could see this man's nose was still slightly crooked. A sudden emotion washed through Cass as he remembered Dustu and his other friends in Echoe. An image of Onacona flashed in his mind, and memories of the good times he had with his Cherokee people as a boy. He spoke again in Cherokee. "Please, come inside and share my coffee."

Dustu told the others to dismount and take a rest on the banks of the Nolichucky while he and Cass spoke privately. Inside the trading post, they shared freshly brewed coffee from a pot on the wood stove and caught up with one another.

Cass was alarmed to learn that Dustu was among those young Cherokee warriors aligned with Dragging Canoe. "The old men want to give our land away. Dragging Canoe stands and fights. Without our land, the Cherokee will be no more," he told Cass.

Cass knew that war parties such as this had been roaming throughout the mountains and valleys on the western edges of white civilization, murdering and scalping men, women, and children. He understood the anger and frustration of men like Dustu, and when he thought about the murder and devastation wrought by the English upon their village and many others, he couldn't blame him. He was curious, though, as to why the Cherokee now seemed to be taking up with the English, who were encouraging them to take the lives of white settlers who were resisting English rule. He asked Dustu about it. "Do you not remember Echoe after that first English attack?"

"I remember. I have no love for any white man, but the English are giving us guns and ammunition to fight these settlers who are breaking the law by moving past the agreed-upon boundary. They are called outlaws by the English. Traitors."

"I have heard them call themselves Americans," Cass told him. "Patriots. I know many who despise the English and want to break away from them. I can understand why the English encourage you to kill them."

Cass also knew that Indians often changed sides in time of war. He remembered how the Cherokee first fought with the French, and then switched to fight for the English in that old war. How they had fought with George Washington and others back then, serving as mercenaries, and not receiving what they considered their due, took out their revenge on innocent settlers in Virginia and North Carolina. He believed that Will's family had been among those murdered at that time.

Although he was glad to see his old friend, their conversation only served to underscore the differences between them. Dustu was all Cherokee, and now Cass was white. "I ask a favor in the name of old friendship," he said as they prepared to part. "My family has moved into the Catawba Valley, alongside the river. Avoid that territory. It is behind the legal boundary, so they are not trespassing on your land."

Dustu agreed to that request, and they parted as friends, although both knew they were now on opposite sides.

* * *

Sycamore Shoals, March 17, 1775

Cass and Jacob Brown arrived at the meeting grounds where the old Cherokee chiefs and many of the tribe had gathered along the banks of the Watauga River. Across the river white settlers looked warily at the crowd of Indians that had grown every day. No one seemed to know exactly what to expect from the day.

They were here to sign a monumental treaty in which the Wataugans were going to purchase outright the lands they had leased several years before. Cass knew Jacob was just biding his time until he could do the same with his property. He had already managed to get more money and trade goods from John McDowell with this intent.

In addition to the leased land, two land speculators, Richard Henderson and Nathaniel Hart, who represented the Transylvania Company, had offered the Cherokees nearly ten thousand pounds in English money and trading goods—mostly guns and ammunition—for the purchase of an enormous tract of land that lay between the Kaintuck and Tanase rivers. Cass knew of Henderson; he was the judge in Hillsborough who had been too cowardly to face and deal with the unruly Regulators and fled in the night. Cass had also heard that Henderson and Hart had hired Daniel Boone to explore the vast territory on their behalf and had already brought in their surveyors to start parceling out the land for sale. He disliked and distrusted Henderson and was sorry Boone, whom he respected, had fallen in with him.

He thought of Dustu and wondered if he was going to be at the gathering. He'd heard Dragging Canoe was expected, and with him could come trouble.

"Look over yonder," Jacob Brown said, pointing to a row of tents. "That's where the goods are on display. Let's go take a look at what it's going to take to get their hands on that land."

The pair rode over to the tents where several Cherokee were curiously surveying the treasure. Cass saw it was stacked to the brim with firearms and ammunition.

"I see now why Attakulakula and Oconostata are eager to make this sale," Cass remarked. "They took a drubbing from some Chickasaws in a recent battle because they ran out of ammunition."

"I just hope Dragging Canoe doesn't get his hands on all this," Brown remarked as they turned away. "All that could be used against the Wataugans and us and any other settler who dares to move west."

Soon a wagon drawn by a team of horses appeared with four riders on horseback. "There's Henderson now," Cass said, recognizing him instantly. The two speculators stepped down from the wagon and were greeted by Attakulakula and Oconostata, and as Cass watched, the four went to the back of the wagon where Henderson broke open a keg of rum. He poured drinks and handed them around, and Cass noted that the Indians drank greedily. It figures, he thought, knowing that Henderson and Hart were plying them with liquor to lubricate the procedure. Did those chiefs even know what they were about to give away?

For a moment, his sympathy was with Dustu and the others who were violently opposed to this sale. He'd also heard that it was illegal for the Cherokees to sell land to anyone but the English crown. But it was apparently a done deal, as the chiefs had met with these two and Daniel Boone earlier to reach terms of the agreement. What was about to transpire now was only a matter of ceremony.

The signing took place under the large sycamores that lined the river, and afterward more rum was shared. Dragging Canoe had not been present as the deal was consummated, but suddenly he appeared with a band of his followers, riding hard into the midst of the crowd. Dismounting, he strode to his father, Attakulakula, a fierce glare on his face. "You have betrayed your people, Father," he accused. "And what you have done is illegal."

Cass saw a frown darken the older Indian's face. "What is done is done, son," Attakulakula replied and turned his back on his son. Then

Dragging Canoe turned to the land speculators and spoke in a voice loud enough for all to hear.

"You've bought a fair land, white man," he said. "But there's a black cloud hanging over it. You'll find its settlement dark and bloody. I, Dragging Canoe, promise you that."

CHAPTER TEN

Catawba Valley, June 1775

Deep in the night, Fiona awoke abruptly with a strong—and terrible—premonition.

Something was wrong with Jeannette. She rolled over and put her feet on the floor to ground her, in case this had just been a bad dream. But the image wouldn't leave her. In her mind, she saw blood. A lot of blood. Jeannette's blood.

"Will!" she roughed his shoulders. "Wake up. We have to go now."

Will bolted upright. "What's wrong?" Instinctively, he reached for his rifle.

Fiona's breath was coming in short gasps. "I...I don't know, but I fear it is Jeannette. Something is happening with her; she is in danger."

Will had witnessed Fiona's intuitive visions many times, and he didn't blink when she told him this. Instead, he pulled on his pants and shirt, donned his boots, and said, "I'll get the horses. You awaken the children."

"Maura and Kate aren't here, remember? They took corn over to the Paterson's yesterday for the mill and planned to spend the night."

"Then get Fergus. Rouse Alicia and Abe."

"Let them come behind us with the wagon. Bring whatever we have to trade for goods there in Salisbury. You and I can't afford a slow journey by wagon."

Fiona awakened Fergus, now twelve, and they went together to the cabin that was home to Alicia and her brother. Quickly, she gave them directions. "We must leave at once on the horses," she said. "At daybreak, load whatever we have on hand to trade, go by the Patersons and fetch Maura and Kate and come on to Salisbury as fast as you can. The mule isn't speedy, but she's steady and strong. Come to Jeannette's. That's where we're going."

Fiona grabbed her old woolen satchel that still held her book of spells and most of the herbs and medicinal plants she found useful in treating neighbors' maladies. Then she and Will mounted their two best horses, ones that were in good shape because Will had trained them and fed them well enough to compete in some of the horse racing that Hunting John and his new neighbor, John Carson, sponsored from time to time. They left in the wee hours of the morning and didn't arrive at Jeannette's until almost dark the following day. Each time they stopped to rest and let the horses graze, Fiona's anxiety grew. Jeannette's lying in wasn't due to begin for three more months, but all her intuition was screaming at her that something had gone badly wrong, and she was delivering the baby too early.

It had all been in a hurry and, thinking back on it as they made their way east, Fiona worried about her children and her African friends. She hadn't heard of any Indian raids in the valley lately, but on a recent brief visit, Cass had told them about the disturbance caused by the young warrior, Dragging Canoe, at the signing of the land sale to whites up in the Watauga area and warned of possible new attacks.

The sun was setting as they pulled up in front of the small parsonage next to the church. A horse hitched to a black buggy was tied to the post out front. Fiona grabbed her satchel and hurried to the door, leaving Will to secure the horses.

Inside, Philemon Means and a man in a dark suit were talking in low voices and turned in astonishment when Fiona burst in. "What is it?" she cried. "What has happened? Is Jeannette alright?"

The two men exchanged glances, and then Philemon introduced the other man. "This is Dr. Barnette," he said. "He has been caring for Jeannette throughout her pregnancy."

Fiona could tell something wasn't right here. "So, where is she? I must go to her."

"She is sleeping," the doctor replied. "I have given her something to ease the pain."

"Pain? What is causing her pain? Is she in labor?"

Again, the doctor exchanged glances with the preacher. "It is over with, madam," the doctor told her. "She...well, she has lost the baby."

Cold fear washed over Fiona, and not waiting further, she rushed toward the one room in the house that appeared to be a bedroom. There on the bed, covered with a quilt, Jeannette lay unconscious. Her face was pale, and blood was seeping onto the coverlet. Fiona threw it back and let out a shriek. "Doctor! Get in here fast! Come now!"

Blood flowed steadily from beneath Jeannette's thin cotton gown. The doctor, followed by Philemon and Will, came into the room, but he looked nonplussed and confused. "She's bleeding again," was all he said. Fiona smelled alcohol on his breath and in an instant knew he was useless.

Furious, Fiona grabbed up the sheet and struggled to staunch the flow. "Get out of here," she growled at the men. "All except Will." The men didn't move for a moment, and Fiona yelled, "Go! Now! Get out! You have done enough damage here. Will, open my satchel and bring me the bottle with the yellow powder in it."

After that, she wasn't aware of anything but saving Jeannette's life. The girl had lost a lot of blood, but she still had a faint pulse. At last, the blood flow stemmed, but Fiona didn't release the pressure on its source. "Where is the babe?" she asked at last to no one in particular. "Where is the afterbirth? What kind of a fool doctor is this man?"

Fiona later learned that Dr. Barnette was the town drunk when he wasn't pretending to practice medicine. But he was the only one in town claiming any medical expertise, and he apparently contributed to Philemon's church. She found it odd that the preacher hadn't called in some of the local women to help Jeannette when she went into premature labor.

To her horror, Fiona found the baby and the afterbirth wrapped in a blanket on the back stoop. She cried as she unwrapped the cold body of the fragile infant. She had seen miscarriages before, but they usually came earlier in the pregnancy. This child was fully formed, if premature.

Jeannette was a healthy young woman. Why would she lose this child after six months? She carried it back inside the house and went directly to Philemon.

"This is your child, sir. It is not some piece of garbage to be disposed of like a turkey carcass. Where is your godliness now? And if Jeannette was having trouble with her pregnancy, why did you not send for me sooner? That man is...he is a poor excuse for a medical doctor. She would have bled to death had I not stopped it. Do you understand me?"

Philemon Means blanched at this torrent from his mother-in-law. "Will she live?" he managed from between white lips.

"If you practice what you preach, I suggest you get over to that church and get down on your knees and pray like you've never prayed before. And make decent arrangements for the child's burial."

The doctor had already left, and the preacher made haste to leave as well, running to the church, whether to pray or to escape her tongue lashing, Fiona wasn't sure. She crept back into the bedroom where Will was keeping vigil over his daughter. When he turned to her, she saw his eyes were red from crying. "I can't lose her," he struggled to find the words. "She is all I have left of..."

"Of Margaret. I know, Will." Fiona had never felt anything but compassion for the woman who had once been Will's beloved wife. "I will do my best to bring her back." She went to the bed and turned back the fresh quilt she'd found and laid over Jeannette. She examined the birth area, which still bled but was no longer a steady flow. Then she moved up to look at Jeannette's belly, and she frowned. "What is this?"

Will was unable to watch what she was doing, so he only replied, "What is what?"

But Fiona made him turn his eyes onto his daughter's pale body. There on her abdomen were dark marks, bruises it looked like to her. "Did that barbarian try to squeeze the baby out of her?" she growled, her anger at the so-called doctor's inept care rising in her again.

"Oh, dear God," Will muttered. "I will kill him for this."

"Let us wait and talk with Jeannette," Fiona said, taking his hand and squeezing it gently.

"When she awakens, perhaps she can tell us what happened."

"If she awakens." Will's voice was dull.

Fiona left Will to keep a vigil over Jeannette, then went into the pantry in search of the makings of a meal. Only then did she realize how weary she was from the long trip and the shock of what had happened. Philemon was nowhere in sight, and again Fiona thought it odd that he hadn't called upon the good ladies of his congregation to at least bring in dishes of food in this time of crisis.

The stores were meager in the parsonage, which again Fiona found strange. After the fine fare Philemon had arranged for their wedding, and knowing Jeannette's skills in the kitchen, it never occurred to her that they wouldn't have a decently stocked pantry. She found a stale loaf of bread and some jam on a shelf, a few eggs in a basket, some cornmeal, and some lye for making soap. There was no dried meat, or vegetables fresh from a garden. In fact, she noted looking out the back of the house, there was no garden. Maybe Jeannette hadn't felt well enough to grow one this year.

She scrambled some of the eggs and managed to find some edible pieces of bread and took them in to Will, only to find he'd fallen asleep in the chair beside his daughter's bed. The sight made her want to cry.

Jeannette appeared to be sleeping peacefully, her breath no longer shallow, and the bleeding was more normal for a woman having recently given birth, so Fiona left them to their slumber and went back into the main room of the house. Philemon still had not returned, so taking a bite or two of the quickly cooling eggs, she put the plate on the table and went to the church. There she found Philemon Means on his knees at the front of the church. The chapel was otherwise empty. She wondered again at the lack of support from the women of the town. In her experience, when there was an illness or tragedy such as this, friends and neighbors were lined up with food and other items of comfort.

Still angry and confused, she turned and left her son-in-law to deal with his grief in his own way. Weariness set in, and she lay down on the bench in front of the fireplace in Philemon's home and fell asleep. She awakened when at last he returned home, but she didn't acknowledge that she'd heard him. From beneath nearly closed lids, she watched him open the bedroom door but quickly retreat when he saw Will. Then without a sound, he slipped back out into the night.

She guessed he would spend the night on a church pew, but at the moment, Fiona didn't give a rat's behind if she ever saw him again.

Chapter Eleven

W ill was with Jeannette when she awoke sometime in the early hours of the morning, and hearing their voices, Fiona got up and went quickly into the bedroom. Jeannette's smile was wan, and her eyes were bleary. "Ma? Pa?" she whispered.

"Shh," Fiona said, going to the bedside and taking the girl's hand. "We're here for you now. Your only job is to regain your strength. Just rest, my darling."

Jeannette rolled her head on the pillow to look at Will. "Pa, I wanted a husband just like you. But..." Her voice caught, and tears shone in her eyes. Then she shut them and drifted off into unconsciousness again.

Will followed his wife from the room and shut the door quietly behind them. "Where's Philemon?" he asked.

"I have no idea. He came in last night briefly, but when he saw you with Jeannette, he left again. He thought I was asleep. I suspect he must have spent the night in his church." She went to the cupboard, and then remembered it was almost bare. "Will, come look at this. They have virtually no food. I'd make us a pot of coffee, but there isn't any."

As soon as the sun was up and the settlement started to stir, Fiona left Will with Jeannette and headed toward a store she remembered was nearby. When she entered, she introduced herself to the shop keeper. "I'm Fiona Gordon, Jeannette Means's mother. She's married to Pastor Means."

The man smiled, but it didn't meet his eyes. "Good morning, madam. How can I help you?"

"I need to purchase some items for their pantry." Fiona selected some bones from a freshly butchered beef to brew into a broth that would restore Jeannette's depleted blood. She also picked up some dried meat. Lard. Butter. Beans. A few ears of early corn. Yellow squash. And flour to make a fresh loaf of bread. When she had finished, she prepared to leave when the store owner stopped her. "That will be one shilling six," he told her.

She looked up, startled. Hardly anyone had currency these days. Exchange was mostly done with barter. "Doesn't the pastor have an account here?"

The man looked embarrassed. "Pastor Means had an account with us. However, he has been unable to pay in many months, so his credit is closed here. I am unfamiliar with you, madam, and you have no account here, so I must ask you to pay for these things. I'm sorry."

Knowing they wanted to purchase supplies while in Salisbury, even in their haste to leave, they'd instructed Fergus, Alicia, and Abe to bring corn meal, salted pork, and some of Will's liquid corn to use as barter for other things they needed, commodities not easily available on the far frontier where they lived. Hurriedly, she explained to the store owner that their wagon was due to arrive in a day or two, bringing goods to exchange for what she needed immediately.

Only when she promised one of their horses as guarantee of payment did he relent and give her what she needed.

She didn't blame the shopkeeper. But as she left the store, she was incredibly curious as to what had gone wrong that the pastor had nothing to pay with, no money and nothing for trade. A congregation usually took care of its preacher in one way or another.

Will was still with Jeannette when she returned, but there had been no sign of Philemon.

"I'd like to tan his hide," Will growled as Fiona handed him a cup of coffee and some bread and jam. "A man should be with his wife at a terrible time like this."

Suddenly Jeannette jerked in her sleep and cried out, then she awoke. This time she seemed more alert than before. She blinked when she saw them.

"Pa? Ma Fiona? What are you doing here? Why..." She looked about her in a daze.

"What happened? Where am I?" And then she started to remember. "Oh. Oh, no, the baby. Where is my baby?"

She tried to sit up, but Will reached over and gently pressed her shoulders back against the feather pillow. Fiona saw the torment and tenderness in his eyes.

Jeannette looked into his face. "I have lost her, haven't I, Pa?"

Will could only nod. "Aye," he said at last. "And we almost lost you."

"Was that horrid Dr. Barnette here?" She shuddered when she said his name.

"Aye," Will said again. "But Fiona made him leave. It was Fiona who managed to stop the bleeding."

"Where...where is Philemon?"

"In the church, praying for you."

At that, a dark shadow crossed her expression. "He should be with his wife. His English God seems not to be listening to him much lately."

Fiona pondered that strange statement for a moment but made no comment. Instead, she turned to Will. "Can you please pour some of the broth that's on the stove into a cup and bring it to us?" To Jeannette, she said, "I have made some broth of beef marrow for you. It will restore your blood. But you must rest and not worry. We will fetch Philemon."

Jeannette said nothing, just turned sorrowful eyes toward her stepmother as her father left the room. "The babe...was it a girl?"

"Aye," Fiona replied, reverting to a word of her youth.

"What...what happened? What have I done that God would take her from me?"

Fiona considered this with interest. They had never been a very religious family, although they attended church whenever services were available. But she supposed that being married to a preacher brought the idea of God into Jeannette's life daily.

* * *

Will brought the requested broth, then excused himself, thinking that they needed time alone for woman's talk. "I'm going to step out for a breath of air," he said.

Closing the front door, he headed straight for the church. There he found Philemon Means puttering around the altar at the front. "Why aren't you with your wife?" Will's voice boomed across the empty church, and Philemon wheeled about. His face was haggard, his eyes red. Will relented a bit, knowing that some men had difficulty dealing with emotional situations like this.

"How is she?" Philemon asked.

"Weak. Tired. She asked where you were."

He seemed surprised. "What else did she say?"

Will thought he caught a note of fear in his question. "Nothing. She nearly died, damn it, she has little strength for talk at the moment."

Philemon nodded. "I must make arrangements for the burial," was all he said. "Since it wasn't born live, there will be no blessing of God on it."

His words rang cold and harsh in Will's ears, and his earlier sympathy turned again to anger. Without another word, he left the church and went back to check on Fiona and Jeannette.

"She's sleeping again," Fiona said as he entered. "She took some of the broth, which is a good sign, but..."

"But what?"

"We only talked for a short while but in her words and manner, there's something...something I can't quite put my finger on. Something akin to fear."

She ladled some of the broth into cups, and the two sat on the bench in front of the fireplace. In June, there was no need for a fire, especially when the house had an iron stove that not only provided for cooking, but also warmed the dwelling adequately. When she took her seat, Fiona looked up at him.

"I'm concerned, Will. Something is not right here." She told him of her visit to the store.

"The storekeeper said that Philemon has been unable to pay him for many months. I know a clergyman makes very little, but I believed his congregation would support him through providing food and other supplies if they had no money to donate."

"Has Jeannette gone hungry?" The thought appalled him. Although he had known many lean times, he had never been truly hungry, and it occurred to him that perhaps if she was malnourished, she had been unable to support the life within her.

"Maybe. I also see she hasn't planted a kitchen garden. That is unlike her. She told me that even as a small child she helped her mother and grandmother plant a summer garden for vegetables and herbs."

"Where is the store?" Will asked. "I need to go and take the horse over to him and find out how much this preacher man owes him, and why he can't pay."

The store was but a short walk, which Will covered in long strides, leading the horse by its reins. With each step, his anxiety grew. Fiona had a way of knowing things, and if she felt even a hint of fear from Jeannette, it was likely there. Maybe the shop owner could shed some light on things.

He entered the store, which was empty of customers, and at first, he saw no one. "Hallo!" he called out. "Hallo the house?" He heard a stirring at the back of the large room and saw an elderly man approaching him. In the dim light, it was hard to make out his features, but something in his gait seemed familiar.

When he reached the front of the store, the man looked up in surprise. "Will? Is that you, Will Gordon?"

"Hiram? Hiram Greenlee?"

CHAPTER TWELVE

W ill was astounded to find his old friend here in Salisbury. The two men started to shake hands, then instead gave each other a hearty embrace. Will stepped back and looked into the wizened face of the older man. "What a surprise! Are you stocking your wagon here, or bringing in goods?"

Greenlee chuckled. "I quit the wagon a few years back, bought this store. Got too dangerous for an old man like me out there with the Indians. I knew many of the older ones, and we trusted one another. But this new generation, I don't know, they're shifty, and they make it plain they hate the whites."

"I've heard the same."

Greenlee indicated for Will to follow him to the rear of the store where benches were placed around a wood stove that was burning only high enough for making coffee. A tin pot sat on the burner. "Can you set a spell?" he pointed to a seat for Will. "We have some catchin' up to do. Coffee?"

"Please."

Greenlee threw out the coarse grounds from an earlier brew and prepared a new pot. "I met up with your son, by the way. Came upon our cabin all cold and wet one wintry day a few years back. I told him if I ever saw you, I'd let you know he was well. Of course, that's been awhile. He seemed able enough to fend for himself, so I hope that he is still hale."

Will assured him that he was, telling Greenlee of the few visits Cass had made to their homestead. "He's something of a loner," he explained. "Speaks fluent Cherokee and has taken up with a man named Jacob Brown who's acquiring land from the Cherokees above the boundary line." He brought Greenlee up to date on the transactions that had transpired earlier that year.

"I heard some of that ruckus," Greenlee said. "Do you remember that medicine woman, Quella? The one who delivered your daughter, what was her name, Jeannette?"

"I only saw her that one night," Will said, taking the hot coffee. "She was there at the birthing. And then she disappeared." He didn't mention that Fiona had known Quella well. He wasn't in the mood to explain her life among the Cherokees.

Greenlee told Will briefly about the strange exchange between Cass and Quella on her last night on earth. "She knew him from his childhood, she said. That night she had some kind of hallucination, said she spoke with his Indian pa, and foretold of some of these troubles that are brewing among us right now."

His last words brought Will back to the reason for his visit. "Speaking of troubles, I hear I owe you for some supplies my wife purchased here earlier today."

Greenlee was surprised. "Your wife?"

"Fiona. Red-headed woman, not very tall."

He saw Greenlee suddenly put two and two together. "That lady is your wife? She said she was Jeannette Means's stepmother." And then it dawned on him. "Jeannette. Is she...your daughter, the one Quella birthed?"

"Aye. She's married to Philemon Means, the preacher at the church over yonder." He added, "I hear he owes you for supplies."

Greenlee scowled. "Means! He's part of the troubles, you know."

"No, I don't know. Please tell me, Hiram, what is going on? My daughter has lost her baby, miscarried late and almost died. Those groceries my wife bought this morning were for her, as there was little food in the house. Why does Philemon owe you?"

Greenlee stared into his coffee cup. "There's strong feelings around here against the English. In fact, the North Carolina Assembly is no longer in service to the king but has become a Provincial Congress. Governor Martin has fled to a British warship down there in Cape Fear. Good thing for him, too. There's many a folk ready to take up arms and run the sons of bitches back across the ocean. Just last month them people over in Mecklenburg County actually declared independence from England after hearing about what happened in Lexington and

Concord up north."

Will was astounded. "Is Philemon one of these men?" Will was puzzled as to how this related to Means's debts.

"Therein lies the problem, Will. Means is a Tory, totally devoted to the king and the Church of England. He preaches weekly about the sins that are being committed by the so-called rebels. He names them traitors, and he encourages everyone in the community to shun them. But his words aren't heeded. In fact, every week, more and more leave his congregation until there aren't many left to support his clergy. Only that old drunk, Dr. Barnette, and a small number of the wealthier citizens. Tories are becoming few around these parts. They are despised, as is Means. I'm surprised somebody hasn't run him off before now."

He looked up abruptly. "Oh, I'm sorry to get off on this, with your daughter's condition and all," he apologized. "I should show more feeling."

"These are the things I need to hear, Hiram. This explains a lot. I fear my daughter's condition was brought about from hunger. Not enough food for that baby. If there is no congregation to support Means, there is no food in the pantry."

"Dear God in heaven," Greenlee swore beneath his breath. "That man. He's an odd one. Hardly ever let his wife out in public, kept her to himself all week, only brought her to church on Sundays occasionally. I'm not sure if any of our women even knew she was going to be a mother."

After leaving Greenlee's store, Will walked the dusty streets of Salisbury, lost in thought and grief. The settlement had grown from the wild and sometimes lawless village it had been when he and Pa Fergus and their families and friends had arrived from Cross Creek. So much had happened in those years. Not all of it good. In fact, he thought bitterly, mostly not so good.

Murders, Indian raids, drought, the Regulation, Cass leaving the family, their own relocation three times now. Had it been worth it?

And now, this business with Jeannette and her husband. He was furious at Philemon Means but at a loss as to what to do about it. He wanted to beat the devil out of him, but he needed to know more. He needed to talk to Jeannette, in private. And he needed Fiona to help him make some sense of all this.

He was concerned as well about the other "troubles" Greenlee had mentioned. Had the people of Mecklenberg actually declared they were independent from the British? It seemed impossible, but Cass had told him of a similar situation with the Wataugans. Living in the outback as they did, they seldom had the opportunity to read newspapers or hear news until it was weeks old. Greenlee had told him of a tavern where the locals gathered to share news and gossip over a pint. Thinking he was of little use to Fiona and Jeannette at the moment, he decided to see what he could learn there.

Like all the buildings in town, the tavern with the unlikely name of the Lilly Belle was rustic and somewhat run-down. A few tables and chairs were scattered about, and a scarred wooden bar stretched across the back of the room. It was early afternoon, but a few men sat at the tables nursing their beer. Will went to the bar and signaled to the tavern keeper. "Got a beer for a thirsty man?" he said with pretended joviality.

"Got money?" the man replied.

Will reached into the pocket of his breeches and came up with two coins. "Will this buy a beer?"

Coins were rare, and the bartender eyed them greedily. "Maybe a couple even. What'll you have?"

Will recalled an earlier visit to a Salisbury tavern. "That German fellow still making his lager around here?"

"Coming right up." When the man had placed the tin mug of beer on the counter and taken one of the two coins, he said, "You new to these parts?"

Will gave him a brief review of how he'd first come to Salisbury, and where he'd been since, but he hadn't come here for small talk. "I'm an old friend of Hiram Greenlee, from his days as a traveling trader."

"Greenlee's a good man," the man said.

"He is that. He's told me about the troubles with the Tories around here, and about that declaration over in Mecklenberg. Wonder where I might get a newspaper or something that will tell me more about what's happening in this world. I live on the edge of nowhere out there on the Catawba. I want to know what's going on."

The man eyed him warily, then motioned to one of the men seated at a nearby table.

"Rutherford, I think there's someone here you need to speak to."

The man named Rutherford stood and came to the bar. "Colonel Griffith Rutherford," he said, extending his hand. "Rowan County Militia." This took Will by surprise, since the man wasn't in uniform, until he remembered that all militia was comprised of civilians.

Will sensed an air of suspicion in the room, and all eyes were on him. "Will Gordon. Have a homestead on the Catawba."

"What can I help you with?"

"Perhaps you can catch me up on what's happening in North Carolina. Hiram Greenlee down at the store told me the governor's fled, and that we have a new Provincial Congress."

"That is true. I'm a member of that Congress, and we've sent a delegation to the Continental Congress in Philadelphia."

Over the next hour and another beer, Rutherford and some of the other men gave Will an earful about the revolutionary activities, both in the north and closer to home. One of the things Rutherford said caught his attention. "The Brits are giving the Cherokees, Creeks, and Shawnees guns and ammunition and encouraging them to kill any white settlers that cross over that old boundary the king set up in '63. Some of those young bucks are eager to lay their hands on white men's scalps, and I've heard the Brits who're paying for them can't really tell where the scalps come from, that side of the line, or this."

The idea made Will's blood run cold. "But I thought the British hated the Indians," he said. "I was with Grant when he moved into Cherokee country and killed hundreds of them, burned their villages."

"That was then, this is now," Rutherford replied wryly. "The British now face a new enemy. We're called Americans. They call us traitors, but we call ourselves Patriots. Tell me, Gordon, are you a Patriot or a Tory?"

Will had never given this much thought, not knowing all this was brewing in a world outside of his small homestead. "I hear you all don't much like Tories around here," he said carefully. "And I care not a lick for the British. Guess you can count me on the Patriot side."

"Then join us. I'm recruiting for our militia." Will hesitated, but before he could speak, Rutherford went on. "Listen, Gordon. Good men and women all over the colonies are fed up with English rules and corruption. Many have already taken up arms. That Mecklenberg declaration isn't the first. Patriots down in Charlestown protested the Tea Act by confiscating all the tea and storing it in their Exchange, and then declared they would be independent from the English from now on. The Continental Congress has not made such a declaration, but I believe it's just a matter of time." He stood up and prepared to leave. "Think about it, Gordon. We're on the edge of freedom now. True freedom! The Patriots have the will, the determination, and the spirit to make it happen. What we need are good men for the fight."

Will left the tavern, his head spinning with the heavy news. A war with England was already begun! General Washington was calling the shots up north, and already had the British surrounded in the city of Boston! The idea was astounding. But now he understood clearly why the citizens of Salisbury were shunning his son-in-law.

CHAPTER THIRTEEN

When he returned to the parsonage, Fiona met him at the door, obviously deeply troubled. "Let's talk out here," she said, indicating two small chairs on the porch. "Jeannette is sleeping."

"Has Philemon showed up?"

At this, Fiona inhaled deeply. "He did. He came in, picked up a few things, took a blanket and some clothes and left. He said nothing, didn't even look in on Jeannette. Will," she said in a low voice, "I think he's left her."

A part of Will sort of rejoiced at the notion, but such a thing was unheard of among decent folks, especially a preacher. "Are you sure? Maybe he is just going to stay over at the church until Jeannette recovers. I sense he doesn't much like us being here."

"Could be, but I followed him. He didn't go to the church. He walked down a couple of streets from here and went into a house. That black buggy that was here last night was tied out front."

"He's gone to stay with that doctor?"

"I don't think so. I waited and watched for a short while, as long as I felt I could leave Jeannette. I went back to the parsonage to check on her, but when I returned to where I saw him last, that buggy was gone. I think they've both left town."

"Does Jeannette know?"

"No. She is recovering, but still very weak. I don't want to distress her further. But...there's more. I went into the church a little while ago, and...Will, that horrid man left the body of their baby on the altar."

Will was sickened. "He told me he was going to make arrangements for a proper burial. I wouldn't say leaving the baby on the altar would count as that."

Will returned to Greenlee's store, told him the facts of the matter, and in a short time, a few of the people who had shunned Pastor Means approached the parsonage. Will stepped out of the front door to meet with them, not knowing what to expect.

"We come to help you bury the child," one man said, removing his hat and holding it to his breast. "Greenlee done told us all about Means's doings, and him leaving town and all. We come to pay our respects to his missus."

A woman stepped forward, her expression sad. "We beg your forgiveness. We didn't know she was expecting a baby. He hid her away, you know."

"I heard that," Will said, coming down the steps, "and we appreciate your help now." He was aware that Fiona had come onto the porch. "My wife and I are deeply grieved that this has befallen our daughter. It would ease her to know the baby is buried respectfully."

The pitiful bundle that had been so cruelly and carelessly handled by its own father was now taken gently from the church and interred in the churchyard behind the building. Later that night, under cover of darkness, Fiona retrieved the putrid afterbirth from the back stoop and buried it according to Cherokee tradition, deep in the woods.

The next day, Jeannette was visibly improved and managed to sit up and take some food. Will and Fiona had told her about Philemon's departure, and the baby's proper burial, but neither seemed to matter much to her. It was as if her spirit had been taken away. Will and Fiona took turns sitting with her, but she was uninterested in talking. She slept a lot. In fact, sleep seemed to come too easily, Will thought.

Fiona assured him that it was common for a woman who'd just given birth to be sad and morose, but especially understandable for one who has lost her baby, and now, it seemed, her husband.

Sitting on the porch together, Will told her all he had learned from Colonel Rutherford, including the new threat to the frontier posed by the British encouragement of the Indians. "He's asked me to join his militia," he said.

"Are you?"

"I don't know. I want to find out if there's a more local militia I can join. I plan to stop by McDowell's on the way home, see what they know." He paused, then admitted, "I hate that I am so ignorant of current affairs. It was embarrassing that I didn't know about this revolution," he said. "Of course, we've heard stirrings about such, but we can't just ignore what's happening and stay isolated out there now. I feel a need to be a part of it."

"I understand," Fiona said quietly. "In the meantime, what are we going to do about Jeannette? If Philemon is truly gone, we can't just leave her here alone."

"I want to take her home, regardless of whether he returns or not."

"He is her husband. I think we should ask her what she wants."

They agreed, and later that afternoon, Will asked Fiona if he could have some private time with his daughter. She, as always, understood.

Jeannette was out of bed and standing by the window. She turned and smiled when he came in. "Pa."

"Shouldn't you be in bed?"

"I'm feeling stronger now, Pa. I think I'm going to be alright."

"Fiona is sure of it. Have you got a minute?" Will realized suddenly what a stupid statement that was. Of course, she had a minute.

Jeannette sat on the edge of the bed. "Seems I have nothing but minutes, Pa. My life is quite empty."

"Fiona and I want to take you home, but if you think you should stay here until Philemon returns, I'll have Alicia come stay with you until then."

"I want to come home, Pa. I don't care if there is a scandal. I won't be near that man again. Ever!" Her vehemence surprised him.

"Want to tell me why?" he probed, hoping to get to the root of her obvious fear.

Tears sprang to her eyes, and she began to cry unashamedly. "Pa, he...he beat me. He would never let me out in town, said I would give the men evil thoughts. He took me to church some Sundays, those times he could make sure the bruises didn't show."

"Dear God," Will swore. "Did he cause those bruises on your belly?"

She looked at him, shocked. "You saw those?"

"Fiona made me look. She thought perhaps that doctor had tried to squeeze the child from you."

Jeannette wrapped her arms around her body, holding herself

tightly, and began rocking back and forth. She wept bitter tears. "He... he said he didn't want this child," she told her father. "He hit me there, again and again. He threw me to the floor. And soon he got his wish. I lost his child."

"Fiona! Come quickly!" Will said, going to Jeannette and holding her tight. "If I ever see that man again, I swear I will kill him on sight."

Fiona hurried into the room. "What's wrong?"

"How soon will she be able to travel?"

"Not for a few more days," Fiona said, watching in concern. "The wagon should arrive any time now. We can bed her down in it, although it will be an uncomfortable ride, I'm afraid."

The wagon didn't arrive for two more days, and Will was almost ready to mount his horse and go look for it when it finally rumbled into town. Behind the reins was young Fergus, his face taut with anxiety.

"Where are the others?" Fiona cried as she dashed down the steps to greet her son. Will was right behind her.

"Ma. Pa." The boy broke down and began to sob. "We couldn't find the girls. We went to the Patersons, like you said, but they said Maura and Katie didn't spend the night like they'd planned. We didn't see them on the way over, so we went back toward our place, but couldn't find them. We figured they might have gotten lost in the woods or something. Alicia and Abe are searching everywhere, but they told me to come on and fetch you."

Lost in the woods. Or something? Will's mind feared the worst. "Can Jeannette travel now?" he asked Fiona.

But Jeannette had come to the door. "Take me home, Pa. Now!"

CHAPTER FOURTEEN

Going over the Blue Ridge, June 1775

Maura clung to the bare back of the man who rode his horse carefully along the narrow trail that led up the steep slope. In front of him, Kate whimpered but had ceased at last to scream.

The small band of Indians had appeared seemingly out of nowhere, accosting the girls as they made their way back home with the handcart filled with cornmeal freshly ground at the Patersons. Kate had cried out, but Maura faced the men without fear.

"Stop. Do not harm us. I am one of you," she said in Cherokee, a language she once spoke fluently but which had become rusty.

One of the men leered at her. "How come you are here with this white girl then?

"She is my sister. My half-sister. My father was Onacona of the Bird Clan. My mother is white. It is not unusual for such a union between the two, is that not so?" Maura knew that many of the white traders and longhunters took Cherokee wives.

The young men looked at one another, perplexed, unsure of what to do with them.

Because they wore no war paint, Maura guessed they were on a hunting expedition in what had always been their traditional territory, but she was also acutely aware of the warnings her brother Cass had given them that there was unrest and disharmony in the tribe, and that the younger men were out hunting for more than wild game. She knew she and Kate might die at their hands, but she resolved to face it bravely.

"Did you ever hear of Unika, great chief of Echoe, and Nanyeh, his wife and beloved woman of the tribe? They are my grandparents." Maura threw this out, hoping to gain more sympathy and thus spare their lives.

"What is your name? Do you have an Indian name?"

"My name is Maura. I was never given an Indian name."

At that, the leader took her by the upper arm and led her to his horse. "Now you will be Leotie, flower of the prairie where I found you, and we will bring you back to our people where you belong."

Before Maura could say more, he signaled for one of the others to hold her while he mounted his horse, then he swung her up behind him. All the time Kate, only three years old, continued to bawl. "What about my sister?" Maura asked, torn between fear and fury. "She is too little to leave alone in the woods. Please leave us both and be on your way."

Instead, the other man lifted Kate to the horse as well, placing her in front of the Indian.

The small party turned and headed toward the high mountains that edged the Catawba Valley. Maura resolved that there was no way out of this, so she took in deep breaths and tried to calm herself. She spoke in English to Kate, attempting to calm her as well.

She dared to ask a few questions of her captor as they rode. She learned his name was Yona, and they were on their way back to his home in the Overhill towns. She had been but four when she was returned to white civilization by Will Gordon, and she had only faint memories of the mention of such a place. She believed it to be over the Tanase River somewhere.

Outwardly calm, inwardly her mind continued wildly to seek ways to escape, or possible sources of rescue. Cass lived up here in the high country. Was there any chance he might come across them and save them? She grieved to think how her mother and Will would suffer when they learned their girls had been taken. Her heart was heavy, and she was afraid, but in an odd way, this going back to the Cherokee seemed natural, since that is where she'd come from. But she was worried about, Kate. A white child with red hair would be at risk, and Maura was unsure what fate lay ahead, for either of them.

After many days of riding, interspersed with the men hunting, the small party reached Yona's village of Chota. Maura was impressed by the size and importance of this town. Yona told her with pride that it was the main capital of the Cherokees, even though individual towns retained their autonomy. Yona took Maura and Kate to the large council house, where he paraded them as his prizes. But old Attakulakula, who was still the highest chief in the nation, scowled.

"You have made a mistake, Yona. This will only anger the white man further. I urge you to return them to their home."

A voice spoke up from a dark corner of the room. "You have made no mistake, brother," Dragging Canoe said, stepping forward. "It matters not if the white man is angry. It also seems not to matter to our old men," he indicated his father, "that we sell our land to them. But it matters to us, the younger ones who have been raised to honor and love this land, as it is our mother. Soon we will strike the war pole against the settlers who call themselves Americans and have renounced the rule of our father, the king of England."

Maura listened carefully as Dragging Canoe continued, speaking in Cherokee. She didn't get it all, but she believed he was outlining plans for Cherokee warriors to fight alongside British soldiers to get rid of all the whites from their ancient lands. "Our English brothers are offering rewards for American scalps. They are bringing guns and ammunition and war supplies soon. And there is more news. Cornstalk of the Shawnee and warriors from other northern tribes are on their way to join forces with us in this war."

The longer he spoke, the greater her fear grew, for herself and Kate, but even more for her family on the Catawba.

They left the council house shortly thereafter, and Yona took the girls to his mother's house. "I have found my wife," he told the older woman. "She is Maura, now called Leotie, daughter of Onacona of Echoe, granddaughter of Unika and Nanyeh. They have all gone to the Great Spirit. Did you know them?"

Maura's eyes widened and she took in a sharp breath. Wife? She hadn't known what to expect, reckoning that if they survived, they'd probably become Cherokee slaves. But married to Yona? She remained silent as the older woman's eyes surveyed her closely. "I knew of them," she replied at last. To Maura she said, "What say you of this marriage?"

"I...I don't want to become Yona's wife," she stammered in her broken Cherokee, fear now filling her entire being. "He has stolen my sister and me from our family over the mountains. I want to go home."

The woman chuckled. "Get over that notion, Leotie. You are Cherokee, you belong with your people."

"My mother is white," Maura said stubbornly. "I am half-breed. And my sister is white. She does not belong here."

"We will not harm the little one," his mother assured her, "as long as you don't try to leave us. Now," she turned to Yona, "take them to the house of your sister. She can make room for them until the ceremony." She chuckled again, and added, "Since her mother is not of us nor among us, there will be no home for you to go to after you are married. I will speak with your father. Perhaps it will be necessary for us to build a new cabin for her."

With that, Yona and his wards were dismissed. The bright sun hurt Maura's eyes as they came out of the dimly lit cabin, and she blinked. She was surprised that tears rolled down her cheeks, as she had not been aware that she'd been crying. Quickly she wiped them away and batted her eyes to staunch them. Kate clung to her hand as if her little fingers had grown attached there. "What place is this, Maura?" Kate asked in a tiny voice. "Where have they taken us? I want my ma and pa. Can we go home now?"

Maura pulled away from Yona's grasp and knelt beside Kate, groping for words that might soften the truth of their predicament— they were prisoners. "This place is a Cherokee village. Do you remember the story Ma told us about how she once went to live in such a place?"

"Uh, not really. Only a little."

"Well, she went to Echoe, another Cherokee town, and married a Cherokee brave. His name was White Owl. I am their daughter. So, I am both Cherokee and white. Can you understand this?"

Kate sobbed and rubbed her eyes. "But my ma and pa aren't Indians."

"No, they are not. And neither is our brother Cass, but he was raised by White Owl and knows the Cherokee ways. You have heard him tell stories when he has visited us. His Indian name is Firehead."

Yona understood enough English to get the gist of what was being said, but his head jerked at the word 'Firehead.'

"You know Firehead?" he asked, pulling Maura upright again.

"Quit that. You are hurting me," she said as she jerked her arm away. "Yes, I know Firehead. He is my brother. Do you know of him?"

Yona spat in the dirt. "Firehead lives with the Wataugans. He is breaking Cherokee and English law by squatting there."

"Firehead has told me he lives mostly in the woods. He is a hunter and trapper. He trades with the Wataugans, but he also has told us he has traded with the Cherokee. In fact, he said an old friend from Echoe, Dustu, recently came to the trading post."

"Dustu? You know Dustu?"

"I don't remember him. I was very young when we left Echoe. We fled when the English destroyed the village. But I think he and Firehead were close friends as children." She paused, then asked, "Do you know Dustu?"

"He lives in Chota now. He follows Dragging Canoe, not the old men."

"Does he despise my brother for making a living trading?" An idea began forming in Maura's mind. Maybe Dustu would take them to Cass.

"I don't know. But he will be interested to learn that you're to be my wife."

Chapter Fifteen

Catawba Valley, July 1775

Fiona knew they would not find Kate and Maura, knew it as sure as anything even before they found the overturned handcart at the edge of the river. Will and Fergus brought it to the wagon and laid it upside down next to where Jeannette sat. Neither said a word.

Alicia and Abe were on the porch of their small cabin, and they ran to the wagon as it approached. Alicia began wailing, and Abe wrung his hands. "They's nowhere to be found, Willgordon," Abe said. He'd been told never to call Will "mastah," but Abe was unable to bring himself to call him by his first name, so he'd always been Willgordon to the young black man.

"We've searched the woods," Alicia said. "No sign of them nowhere."

Will helped Jeannette down from the wagon bed, and Fiona took her arm. She was shaky from the long hard journey, but the extreme bleeding had not reoccurred, so Fiona believed that time would heal all the wounds the girl now suffered. "Jeannette's come home," was all she said to Alicia and Abe. "Help me get her into the girls' room."

"I can't take their room," Jeannette protested weakly.

"Yes, you can," Fiona said. Her heart was torn to admit to herself that the girls wouldn't be needing it, at least not any time soon.

She instructed Alicia to cook up something for them to eat and to keep an eye on Jeannette, whose depression deepened at learning her sisters had disappeared. Fiona went back outside. The day was hot, and clouds piling up to the west portended one of the frequent summer afternoon storms in the mountains. She found Will leaning against one of the porch supports. His head was down, and his whole body sagged in sorrow. She went to him and gently touched his arm.

"Jeannette's settled in," she murmured, not knowing what else to say. He had just lost two daughters, and Jeannette had almost died. How much more could a father take? Fiona herself was desolate and in despair. Those were her natural born daughters. She feared for their lives, and yet something told her they were not in danger of being killed—yet.

"They've taken them," Will said at last. "The Indians have taken our girls." He didn't try to disguise his anguish. Instead, he turned to Fiona and encircled her in his arms, and he buried his tears in her thick hair. They stood together for a long while, weeping until no more tears would come.

"I have some dinner ready." Alicia's timid voice cut through the warm summer air.

Fiona straightened and took Will's hand. "It's been a long journey, Will. We need to eat something, and then we can try to think of what to do next."

Will and Fergus went into the cabin and took seats at the table. Fiona called Abe in for dinner and helped Alicia serve up the biscuits, bacon, corn, and mugs of buttermilk, but no one had much appetite. Fergus, who at twelve was always hungry, at last ate a biscuit. "Are we going to go hunt for them, Pa?" he asked.

Will heaved a sigh and wrapped a biscuit around some bacon. "Yes, of course. But I'm trying to think. There are only two horses, and they're worn from the trip. The girls have been missing for nearly a week. If they left the Patersons that afternoon instead of spending the night, they should have been home before we ever left. So, whatever happened to them, happened that afternoon. We likely passed that handcart in the night as we left."

"They could be anywhere in these mountains," Fergus offered, not realizing the terrible impact of this truth. "Maybe we should go try to find Cass."

"I'm thinking we round up as many of our neighbors as we can and go on an Indian hunt ourselves." Will suddenly had blood in his eyes, and she knew the fire she'd suspected had long burned inside this quiet man was about to rage out of control.

* * *

Families from throughout the Catawba Valley, now newly alarmed for their safety, searched the valley and mountains as far as the top of the Blue Ridge, but no trace of the girls was found. The only hopeful sign was that they had not found their bodies either. Fiona appreciated the perseverance of the searchers, for they combed the woods for the rest of the summer, but she held herself together with a feeling deep inside that her children were alive, somewhere, and would return, someday. She kept the stone talisman close at hand, and as the days passed and the search produced nothing, it received many hours of attention from her fingers.

She worried most about Will, and for his sake, refused to weaken her resolve not to give into despair. He became more haggard with each disappointing foray, more withdrawn. One day she awoke to find him gone. A note on the table said simply, "Going to find Cass. Be safe."

Winter was upon them before he returned, without their son. "He wasn't at Watauga," he told her. "I left word with that Jacob Brown fellow for him to come home, told him what had happened, and that we needed him here. Apparently, he's gone off on a hunt with Boone and some others over in Kaintuck."

Jeannette and Fergus both struggled to maintain a good face, but Fiona saw Jeannette kneeling by her bed each night and heard her prayers for the safe return of her sisters. She had regained her health, if not her old spirit. She moved remotely through the days, diligent in her help on the farm and in the house, but not once did she show much enthusiasm for living. It broke Fiona's heart, for she had always been a lively girl.

Even Alicia and Abe were forlorn, although Alicia had developed a keen interest in a man who worked on Joseph McDowell's farm. His name was Billy, and he was a slave, like all the McDowell workers, but he was an odd one, in looks at least. His skin was not dark, swarthy but not black. His eyes were blue. His hair was curly, but not the tight black kinks of the other blacks. Once on a visit to their place, Joseph's wife, Margaret, told her that at the slave market, they'd called him a Melungeon, but she had no idea what that meant.

In the spring, although the idea of slavery was repugnant to him,

Will purchased Billy, and shortly thereafter, Alicia married him. Fiona was happy to have Billy with them, not only for Alicia's sake, but also that there was another man on their farm. Billy proved to be a hard worker, and he was a crack shot, another comforting aspect of his presence.

Abe, too, found a wife shortly thereafter, a young slave named Cissy, and Will purchased her from Colonel John Carson, an Irishman who was garnering land up near Hunting John's place. Abe and Cissy added more stability to their homestead, and even though Billy and Cissy were slaves, they were treated as part of the family, as Alicia and Abe had always been.

Fiona and Alicia were delighted that Billy brought with him a stringed instrument he called a banshaw. "Ngoni!" Alicia had exclaimed when she first saw him play it at a dance at the McDowell's place, and Fiona remembered that this was her native African word for a similar instrument she had played at Edgewater. In fact, Fiona thought it might be part of the reason Alicia had fallen for Billy when until now, her African friend had shown little interest in men.

As the weather warmed and the crops were planted, everyone's spirit improved and, in the evenings, Fiona brought out her fiddle, and Billy played his banshaw. Will looked on but didn't pick up his fiddle. Neither did Jeannette's feet tap out the rhythm as she once had done.

It was on just such a night that a lone rider approached. It was moonless and overcast, but Fiona saw there were two figures on the horse. Then she heard the voice of a very young girl.

"Ma!" Kate cried, and Cass spurred their mount toward the cabin at a trot.

CHAPTER SIXTEEN

Brown's Trading Post, April 1776

Cass had been away most of the winter exploring the land beyond the Cumberland Gap with Daniel Boone and others who were busily surveying the property for future sale. He still had mixed feelings about the legality of the purchase by Richard Henderson, but he found excitement in exploring a new hunting ground. When he returned to Brown's Place, Jacob was gone on his own hunting trip. He had returned only yesterday.

Brown had apparently not done a lot of blacksmithing while he was away, and Cass found a lot of work waiting for him. He was at his smithy shaping an iron tool for one of the Wataugans when three horsemen rode into the small settlement. He recognized them as traders who had yards in the Cherokee capital of Chota. He put aside his hammer and laid the tool across a tree stump.

"Mornin', fellas," he greeted them. "What can I do for you?"

They dismounted and tied their horses. "Got coffee?" one of them asked as he secured the laden pack horses that accompanied them. "Been a long ride over here."

Cass invited them to join him next door at the trading store, and they made small talk while the coffee brewed. But Cass was curious. It appeared that they were leaving the area with trade goods instead of bringing them in. "You bringing those goods to trade here?" He poured the hot coffee into four tin cups and handed one to each trader.

"Nope," replied one of them, Jarrett Williams. We're taking some of our goods back into Virginny to store in case there's troubles out here."

That had Cass's immediate attention. The settlers west of the Blue Ridge, believing they now owned their land, remained nervous about the Indian unrest stirred up by Dragging Canoe.

"What's up?"

Isaac Thomas, a weathered older man who Cass knew was respected among both Indians and whites, said, "That damned Dragging Canoe has a bit between his teeth to go to war and kill all the white folks who've moved out here. Their *giga-hyuh*, their Beloved Woman Nancy Ward, speaks against the fighting, but he just won't let it go. And his English 'brother,' the one he calls Scotchie, and that other one Stuart, are egging him on."

Williams spoke up again. "Rumor has it that some northern Indians are on their way to Chota to get the Cherokee to strike the war pole with them and fight together for the English king."

The third man, William Fawling, snorted. "The king. Their 'Father,' they call him."

Cass had been uneasy since the day he'd witnessed Dragging Canoe's angry speech at Sycamore Shoals. "I thought the Cherokee were enemies of those tribes, especially the Shawnee."

"That has been their tradition, but now even Dragging Canoe can see that the tribes must band together or be defeated. Pretty savvy of him if I say so myself." Isaac Thomas shook his head. "If this comes to pass, all the white settlers from Virginny clear down to Florida that are movin' west better get ready for a bloody fight. That's what we're doing. We're thinkin' it's better to move our trade goods further into Virginny than leave them out here where Dragging Canoe and his young hotheads could confiscate them. This is probably the first of a number of trips it'll take, because we want to do it all slow-like so they won't suspicion what we're doing."

"Have you warned anybody about this, besides me?" Cass asked.

"Not yet. You're our first stop. We'll spread the word to whoever we come across on our trip, but if'n I was you'uns, I'd start buildin' some forts up here. Or finishin' th' ones you got started. Or," Fawling paused and gave Cass a wry grin, "you could get all these white folks to leave everything and head back over the mountains and be good children again to that ole king."

"Ha," Cass said, pouring more coffee into their cups. "We all know that'll never happen."

"Better git going now," Fawling said. "Want to make as much time as we can in daylight."

The three returned to their horses, but before Thomas mounted up, he said, "By the way, in case anyone's looking for some missing girls, a hunting party brought a couple of them into Chota last summer. Kidnapped from over the mountains, they said."

"Know who they are?" Cass asked, a sudden premonition washing over him. "Where'd they come from?"

"Older one looks Indian, although they say she's half-breed. They call her Leotie now, and she's been made to marry the Indian who took her. Name's Yona. The other is a little girl, four or maybe five years. White, with a mop of red hair and bright green eyes."

"Those sons of bitches," Cass swore, slamming his tin cup onto the stove top. "I know those girls. They're my sisters."

* * *

The traders had barely gone on their way when Cass ran to find Jacob Brown, who hadn't shown his face yet this morning. Cass pounded on Brown's cabin door. "Brown! Wake up!"

The older trader showed up in breeches held up with suspenders over a thin undershirt. "What's the matter? Why you come getting me out of bed like this?"

Cass didn't bother to point out that it was already past nine o'clock. "I have to go, Jacob. Going to Chota. I think those damned Indians have kidnapped my sisters."

"Whoa! Hold on just a minute. What are you saying? How'd you hear that?"

Cass rattled out the stories the traders had told him, not only about the kidnapping, but also about the looming threat. "Jacob, make yourself useful and ride to the other settlements and those out on farms and let them know what's happening. Or could happen."

Brown looked somewhat befuddled, and Cass suspected he might be hung over. But then the old man said, "I fear you are right. I hadn't seen you to tell you this, but your pa was through here last winter lookin' for them. Said to tell you they'd been kidnapped."

Cass felt as if someone had hit him in the belly. So, it was true! Maura and Katie in the hands of Indians who were threatening to murder all whites. Good God, were they even still alive?

There was only one way to find out.

* * *

Cass was greeted at the edge of the village by a pack of barking dogs and the curious stares of the natives. His face was set, and his demeanor was grim. "Take me to Attakulakula," he said to a small boy. Best to go straight to the old chief, whom he knew was sympathetic to the white man. He guided his horse behind the boy, who took him not to the council house but rather to a large cabin similar to the one that had been his own home back in Echoe. The boy shouted something in Cherokee, not knowing this white man with the red hair could understand.

"White devil is here!" he shouted, then dashed away to stand a few yards distant. A small crowd had gathered.

Presently a bent older man emerged and squinted up at Cass. "You come in peace?"

Cass nodded. "I did. I came for my sisters. I believe your men kidnapped them last summer. Maura and Kate. Are they here?"

He saw the old man's shoulders visibly slump. "I knew there'd be trouble," the chief mumbled. But he beckoned Cass to dismount and follow him.

Heart pounding, Cass took his rifle in hand and reluctantly left his saddle. He walked respectfully behind this man whose reputation as a peacemaker was known throughout the frontier. He was the famous Attakulakula, the Little Carpenter, they called him because he'd proven to be proficient at carving out details of treaties and agreements as would a skilled carpenter piece together wood.

They stopped at a cabin at the far western edge of the town. "Yona!" the old chief called in a surprisingly strong voice. "Yona! Come now! You have a visitor."

A young warrior appeared from around the back of the cabin. "What is it, old man?" His tone was disrespectful. Then he spotted Will. "Who are you?"

"I am brother of Maura and Kate, the girls you kidnapped last summer. I came to take them home. Peacefully," he added, but wondered if that was a possibility. Suddenly he hoped he hadn't made a mistake. Would they hand over the girls, whom he hadn't yet seen or have any proof they were in the village, or would they take him prisoner? Possibly kill him? He hoped that being at the side of the old chief would insure him against harm, at least until he left, with or without the girls.

The door to the cabin opened, and Maura stepped out into the afternoon sun. "Cass?" she said and ran to him. He held her close and thought he might cry for joy at seeing her and that she was safe. Then rough hands jerked her away from him.

"You don't touch my wife," Yona barked. "Leotie is mine now."

Cass gulped. Wife? He turned to Maura. "Is it true? Are you married to this man?" But the truth was evident in the swelling of her belly.

She looked at her brother. "It is true, Cass. I am now Leotie, wife of Yona, and at home with my Cherokee people." Her voice was calm and even, and as was her way, her expression inscrutable.

"Your people are Ma and Pa," Cass said quietly. "You don't belong here, Maura. I've come to take you home.

She gave him a patient smile. "You don't understand, brother." She reached for Yona's hand. "He is my husband. He has been good to me, and I have fallen in love with him. This is my home now," she repeated. "I hope you will try to get Ma and Pa to understand. Ma might, since she too was once married to a Cherokee."

Cass was nonplussed. It hadn't occurred to him on his journey to save her that Maura might not wish to return with him. But he also knew the conflicting emotions he'd had about his identity—whether he was white or Cherokee—and he understood how she must have felt being taken away from her Cherokee home into white civilization where people had not always been kind. "Where's Kate?" he asked.

Maura turned to Yona and said in Cherokee, "Please, get her and bring her here. We must let her go if that is what she wants."

CHAPTER SEVENTEEN

Catawba Valley, Late April 1776

Fiona could scarcely believe her eyes when she saw Cass and Kate racing toward them. Maybe Jeannette's prayers had been heard. She ran across the open field, and Cass reined in the horse. Kate squirmed out of her brother's arms and jumped down.

"Ma! Oh, Ma," and then she began to cry.

Will was right behind Fiona, and he took the horse's reins. "Cass, I've never been so glad to see anyone in my life. I guess Jacob gave you my message."

"He did, but not until last week," Cass said, dismounting. "I've been gone all winter, and so has he. Some traders came through from Chota and told me about a couple of hostages, girls who'd been taken from someplace over the mountains."

"There were a couple," Will said, picking up little Kate and holding her tight. "Where's Maura?"

Cass didn't answer. Instead, he embraced his mother. "Let's go inside. Got any supper? We're starving."

Fiona was overjoyed that Kate had been rescued, but she dreaded to learn of Maura's fate. Jeannette and the others had rushed toward them, and all were shouting excitedly and talking at once as they made their way into the warmth and light of the cabin. Alicia and Cissy quickly made plates of food for the new arrivals, and the two ate in silence for a few minutes, devouring the ham and beans with relish.

"I have news of Maura," Cass said at last, but Kate usurped him.

"She married Yona," she blurted. "She's not coming back."

It took a long moment for this to sink in, but Fiona was only half surprised by the news. She remembered the look of longing on Maura's usually impassive face when she had stared across the river at the Indians back when they came to sign the land leases over at Hunting John's. She'd known then that Maura missed her Cherokee home.

"Can you tell us what happened the day the Indians took you and Maura?" Will asked Kate gently. Turning to look at him, Fiona could tell he was shaken by this news.

"They came out of the woods, Pa, when we were coming back from Paterson's mill. I was scared, but Maura was brave, and she could speak to them in their words."

"How many were there?" Will asked.

"Four, I think. Yona said we were wrong to be on their hunting grounds, and so they took us away."

Fiona let out a breath. "But they didn't harm you, did they?"

Kate shook her head. Her hair had grown long and was wild and fiery like her mother's.

"No. They didn't say much either. We just rode along. At night they built a fire, and we ate what they killed that day."

"Didn't Maura try to run away?" Cass asked.

"They said if she tried, they would kill us both and take our scalps back to their village."

Fiona was horrified that this child who was barely five years old knew about such things as killing and scalping. What else had she seen while she was at Chota?

Kate laid her head on the table after Cissy cleared the plates away, and her eyelids drooped. "Let's get her to bed," Fiona said softly.

"She can sleep with me," Jeannette said, and Fiona saw a glimmer of the spirited girl she once knew. Jeannette smiled over at Fiona. "After all, it was her room before it was mine."

With Kate tucked in and already sound asleep, Jeannette came back across the dog trot and into the main cabin. Cass was being introduced to the new blacks who had become part of their homestead in his absence.

When Jeannette took a seat by the fire, Fiona could stand it no longer. "Tell me about Maura. Is it true she's married the Indian who kidnapped her?"

Cass drew in a deep breath. "It is, Ma. I saw her in the village when I went to fetch them. She...she is with child already, I could tell."

Fiona's heart broke just a little more, but she only nodded for him to go on. "I met this man, Yona. He's...well, he seemed right enough. I tried to get Maura to leave and come with me, but Ma, she said she loves Yona, and that she feels like she belongs with the Cherokees."

Later, Fiona and Will sat alone in the two chairs on the porch, each lost in thought. At last Fiona spoke. "I can understand her, Will. She is half Indian, and she was always happy back at Echoe, even though she was only a child when we left."

"I just hope they don't harm her," Will said. "You know what Rutherford told me about the English goading the Indians to kill white settlers in this new war."

"If she loves this Yona, and has chosen to remain with him, I trust that she will be protected...unless," she paused, "there is some kind of invasion of their town, like happened to us twice at Echoe."

Will was silent, and Fiona guessed he was remembering his own part in destroying Indian villages. She filled the silence, saying, "Maura is nineteen now. Marriageable age. But I haven't seen any of our neighbor boys come courting. Because she's part Indian, and she looks it," she added, somewhat bitterly. "Maybe she's right, Will. Maybe she is exactly where she belongs, with the Cherokee, and with a husband she apparently loves. She will soon have a baby with more Indian blood than her own."

"But..."

"No buts. You forget I too once loved a Cherokee. And I was surrounded by some kind and caring people." She laid her hand on his. "Not all Indians are bad, Will. Just like not all white people are good. She is gone from us now, and I know we may never see her again." She sighed. "Now I know how my own Da and Granny felt when I left. But they bade me go, thinking it was best for my life, and now I must do the same with Maura."

And then she couldn't help it. Fiona started to cry.

Chapter Eighteen

Chota, Cherokee Territory, May 1776

Leotie's heart had been torn as she watched Cass and Kate leave the village that day, accompanied by Yona and two other braves. She'd made her husband promise to escort them safely back to Brown's Place, and she believed he had honored her wishes. There had been no report of killings in the area since that time.

She understood her brother's anguish at her decision to remain with the Cherokee, but in her heart, she knew it was right. She loved her Ma dearly, and Pa Will as well, but she had never felt totally at home in the white man's world, where she was often called derogatory names, both to her face and behind her back. Injun. Nigger squaw.

Here she had found her place. It was as if she had never left a Cherokee village. She'd been treated kindly by Yona's mother and sisters and had met a woman she now idolized, Nancy Ward, a Cherokee woman married to a white trader, who seemed to understand Leotie's desire to return to their world.

Nancy was the *Giga-hyuh* of this tribe, the Beloved Woman whose voice was listened to by all in the village. She had earned this place of honor as a warrior who'd fought beside her first husband in a battle against the Creeks. He was killed, but she took over his weapon and fought bravely until they were at last victorious. Now, she carried the white swan feather of the Beloved Woman, and it was clear from what Leotie had heard in the council house, she was of like mind with old Attakulakula, her uncle, wanting to avoid war with the white settlers.

"Many Cherokee women have husbands among the whites," she'd said. "They have their children. If you go to war against them, you will be fighting against your own families. It is time for you, Dragging Canoe, my cousin, to hold the peace. You must remember the ancient tradition of listening to the voices of the women."

But Dragging Canoe and his followers were not interested in her words, or her advice.

Yona had told Maura that Dragging Canoe was anxious for the arrival of the large delegation of Indians from northern tribes who were traveling to greet their southern brothers in hopes of forming a united front against the white settlements that kept moving ever westward.

Leotie had spoken with Yona about the two factions that had split the Cherokee nation, the peacekeepers and those who wanted nothing more than a war to annihilate the whites. She worried that he was among the latter, although he kept his thoughts mostly to himself. She had heard Dragging Canoe make his speeches before the council, and never had she seen anyone with more venom and hate in his heart. She was glad little Kate had been safely rescued, or she might have been killed and scalped by one of these hotheads. As Yona's wife, Leotie didn't fear for her own safety, but she wondered about the white traders who lived here at Chota, including Nancy's husband, Bryan Ward.

For days ahead of the arrival of the delegation from the north, the entire town and even some of those in nearby villages scurried to prepare for the accommodation of their visitors.

Food was gathered from whatever resources they had, although it was early in the year for the harvest. There was high excitement in the air, and even Yona, who tried to hold himself aloof and impassive when speaking of the troubles with the whites, joined in the preparations.

The northern delegation arrived in full regalia, led by the Shawnee high chief, Cornstalk.

Among them were Shawnees, Delawares, Mohawks, Nancutas, and Ottowatas. They were allies of the king of England, and British loyalists up north had urged them to join with one another, including the Cherokee, against the Americans. For several days, Leotie and the citizens of Chota and surrounding Cherokee villages hosted feasts and dancing in welcome.

And then they got down to the business of their visit. Leotie and Yona went with all the others into the large council house to hear what they had to say. Old Attakulakula and others made formal speeches of welcome, and then Cornstalk, tall and regal in his white shirt of English make with lace cuffs and collar, stood and commanded everyone's attention. Over his shirt he wore a British military red coat, and a British saber dangled at his side.

His message, spoken in a strong clear voice, was a plea for the help of the Cherokee in supporting the king over the rebels calling themselves Americans. "The Great King, our Father," he boomed, "needs our help. Some of his children have turned against him, and they no longer recognize his law." A murmur of approval stirred through the gathering, especially among those who followed Dragging Canoe.

Leotie touched Yona's arm. "Are you with these warriors?"

But he gave her no answer.

She watched as several of the visitors displayed long war belts. Cornstalk offered one to Attakulakula, who only looked away, as did Oconostata. Cornstalk approached the *Giga-hyuh*, but she, too, turned away. Then Dragging Canoe boldly stepped forward and held out his hands, and the war belt was passed to him. The young warriors let out whoops of glee and in turn accepted war belts from others of the visiting delegation. And then the war dances began.

Leotie left the meeting with Nancy Ward, who was so distressed she was almost in tears. "I have friends and family who will be killed, and for no reason other than to satiate the blood lust of those young bucks," she told Leotie.

Yona was nowhere to be found, and later Leotie learned he had gone with Dragging Canoe and some of the others over to the Watauga settlement. The following day, the small raiding party returned bearing four fresh scalps on a wooden ring. Dragging Canoe handed them to Cornstalk as the Indians were about to leave. "Accept these as a token of our alliance," he said to the Shawnee chief. "We Cherokees are with you in fighting the Americans."

"So you are with him?" Leotie demanded of Yona when at last he returned to their cabin. "Why do you not listen to the advice of your elders?"

Yona made a face. "Those old men should move on to the Great

Spirit," he said with distain. "Their trust in white men has only led to more destruction of our people."

"So now you're willing to fight for a white king you've never seen? Yona, I've told you before, it was the king's men who invaded our towns and killed hundreds of our people. Why would you support him now?"

"Because, my Leotie," Yona said, taking her face in his hands, "Dragging Canoe is right. The king's army is our only chance at making a stand against these white settlers. It is a strong army, and with our help and that of our other Indian brothers, we stand a chance of ridding our nation of these invaders forever. Otherwise, our people will be wiped out."

With that, Yona left their cabin and made his way back to where Dragging Canoe, the Raven, and Abram of Chilowhee were gathered, discussing their role in the attacks planned along the frontier by the Indian alliance. Leotie rubbed her hands across her belly, wondering if she'd made a mistake in not crossing back into the white man's world with Cass. She agreed with Nancy Ward that the Indians' cause was without hope, and now her husband, whom she had grown to love, was like a stranger. Her heart wept.

Ammunition provided by the English arrived in Chota, a hundred wagon loads that Dragging Canoe immediately confiscated. Warriors began to gather, painting themselves black and fasting in preparation for the fight to come. Leotie watched in fascination and horror as they danced throughout the nights the War dance and the Brave dance, wearing wooden masks carved with rattlesnakes on the top. More fearful than she'd ever been since arriving in Chota, Leotie sought out Nancy Ward.

"What are we to do?" she asked the Beloved Woman.

"We cannot stop them, and I, as the *Giga-hyuh*, must prepare the traditional black drink to purify them before war."

Leotie followed her to the council house and watched as she brewed up a potion that the warriors would later drink. Later, the two women sat together next to the warriors and the headmen. It was there Nancy learned of their plan of attack.

After the ceremonies, Nancy took Leotie's hand and drew her outside. "Come quickly!" she whispered. "There's something we must do."

The older woman, who in Leotie's mind was now something of a big sister, bid her to follow, and the two made their way to the trading yards. There, the three traders who had already begun to reduce their inventory by taking it in small quantities over to safer territory in Virginia, were gathered, talking in low voices about what Dragging Canoe had told them—they could either join in the fighting, or if they chose not to, they would be expected to supply his warriors with their goods.

"I don't like this business none," one of them said. "We need to get out of here."

Nancy and Leotie startled them at their approach. "*Siyo!*" Nancy greeted the men, whom she obviously knew well. And then she proceeded to reveal Dragging Canoe's plan to attack three settlements— Watauga, Holston, and Carter's Valley—simultaneously, with different warriors leading each party.

"You must ride now, tonight!" she urged them. "Warn these people to make haste to safety, or terrible blood will be shed!"

She and Leotie helped the three traders quietly disappear into the night. Then Nancy turned to Leotie. "I have trusted you, little sister, because I believe you feel as I do and are friend to both whites and Indians. You must speak of this to no one, not even your husband." She paused, then added emphatically, "Especially not your husband. Go to him tonight and give him comfort, for when he rides out with Dragging Canoe, he may not return."

CHAPTER NINETEEN

Brown's Trading Post, July 1776

One of the traders who had passed through the Watauga settlements earlier transporting some of their goods back into Virginia showed up unexpectedly in the night with a renewed warning. "You'uns better have those forts built by now," he said, "'cause them Indians is comin' your way in no time atall."

He told Cass and Jacob Brown the Indians' plan of attack, then moved on to warn other settlers. Cass and Jacob made a hurried plan, with Jacob gathering up all the folks nearby and going to Fort Caswell. Cass was to ride hard over to the Sevier's place and make sure they got the word. As he mounted his horse, he wondered if Fort Lee, the one they had been building, was finished yet.

He rode through the dark night to Plum Grove where John Sevier and his family lived. It was not yet dawn when he reined in, but the household was already astir.

"Haloo, John! Sarah! Haloo!" he shouted, and a tall man stepped onto the porch. Several children spilled out the door after him, curious about their early morning visitor.

John Sevier was well known in these mountains as an Indian fighter and a man who was fiercely devoted to defending the freedom of settlers to move westward. He was a proud man, a local farmer who had by this time fathered eight children. He was among those appointed to administer the Watauga Association a few years back, a first step toward breaking free of the British. Just last year, when the Wataugans learned of the outbreak of the American War for Independence, he helped reorganize the area into the Washington District which declared loyalty to the United Colonies, not the king. As in other colonial areas, thcy formed a Committee of Safety as their governing body, and they requested annexation by the state of Virginia. It was declined, so plans were afoot to make the same request to North Carolina. This was all far from Cass's mind, however, as he began spreading the word of the ensuing Cherokee attack.

"Fort Lee is not nearly finished," Sevier told him over coffee and a hot breakfast. "When do you think the attacks will come?"

"Isaac Thomas wasn't sure, but he believes it will be within a week or so."

Sarah Sevier laid her hand on her husband's shoulder. "We must go to Fort Caswell," she told him. "It's not worth completing the new fort at the risk of all of our lives."

When Cass arrived at Fort Caswell, which had been built last year on the shoals of the Watauga River, he found himself among almost two hundred settlers who had fled there for safety. It was in the dead heat of summer, and the crowded conditions were miserable. For the most part, he heard no real grumbling, just a desire to meet the enemy and get this over with.

Many head of cattle, including milk cows, had been herded to the fort to provide food for the refugees but had to be pastured outside the walls. As days went on and no attack came, some of the women ventured out to milk the cows, as their supplies were being taxed by the numbers to be fed. But one morning in late July, the women were surprised and out in the open when Old Abram of Chilhowee led the Cherokee attack against the fort. Some of them made it to the safety of the walls, but one was shot dead. One young woman, who later Cass learned was named Catherine Sherrill, was unable to get to the fort before the gates swung shut and were locked against invasion.

Cass was among those atop the parapet with rifle in hand, shooting at the advancing enemy, and he was astonished to see John Sevier being lowered head-down over the side of the wall. He took a chance and looked over the palisade to see what was happening and saw Catherine Sherrill run and jump toward Sevier's extended arms. Through some miracle, neither received a Cherokee bullet, and the young woman was hauled to safety.

Cass returned his attention to the attack, taking careful aim, reloading quickly, and bringing a number of Indians to the ground.

Then he heard, "Fire!" Again taking a chance, he peered over the wall and saw Indians with firebrands trying to burn the fort. He took a shot at them, then ducked his head back. Below, he heard a commotion, and as he reloaded his rifle, he looked down into the fort. There he saw a woman grab a bucket and dip it into the wash water that had been boiling before the attack. She then scaled the ladder to the top of the palisades, signaled for the other women to hoist the bucket up, and fearlessly, she leaned over the side and poured the scalding water on the Indians. She was hit by a bullet, but not before several more buckets went onto the Indians. Her water put a stop to the effort to burn the fort, and her courage seemed to galvanize all who saw what happened.

Soon after, the shooting stopped. All grew ominously quiet as the contingent of refugees held their collective breath and listened for sounds of a renewed offensive. But none was forthcoming. Cass sat on the parapet and leaned against the palisade, his heart pounding. The women of the frontier were a far cry from those he'd met in Hillsborough, he thought. These were as tough and determined as the men. And just as brave, if not more so.

James Robertson, the commander of the fort and brother to the woman who'd poured the water on the attackers, believed they were now under siege. "We didn't rout them," he said, "even though we gave it a good run. They're still out there, and they know if they keep us in here, sooner or later we'll run out of provisions. They have the forests, fields, and our cattle to supply their fighters. We have only what we could bring into these walls."

Days crept by, and boredom set in. Boredom laced with anxiety. A few foolhardy souls did venture outside, however, and two of them were captured, a young boy and a woman named Lydia Bean. The Beans were among the earliest settlers on the Watauga, and her capture hit the cooped-up community hard. Frustration and fear led to discord among even the most cordial neighbors, and Cass heard one of them vow to go back east if he ever got out of here alive.

They did get out alive. Two weeks into the siege, it appeared that

Old Abram and his raiders had disappeared. Robertson cautiously sent scouts into the woods, including Cass, but all they found were the blackened circles where their campfires had been, and trampled undergrowth. Cass did not return to Brown's Place right away but stayed at the fort to defend it again should they be mistaken that the siege was over.

* * *

Chota, late July 1776

Two of the three raiding parties returned to Chota, many of the warriors wounded, others carrying the dead. Yona and two others carried Dragging Canoe and his brother, both of whom were shot, into the council house at Chota, where Nancy Ward, Leotie, and other women bound their wounds and gave them herbal medicines to keep the infection away.

"They knew we were coming," Dragging Canoe growled, and he looked Nancy directly in the eyes. "Someone warned them."

Nancy's face remained impassive, but Dragging Canoe knew his cousin had betrayed him. Leotie wondered if he would try to take revenge on his own kin.

When she returned to her cabin, Yona was not there. She was anxious to talk to him and hear what had taken place, so she wandered through the village looking for him. She found him standing alone at the edge of the woods, peering into the darkness of the forest.

"What is wrong, my husband?" she said, approaching him quietly.

He turned and frowned. "Everything is wrong," he said, his words a mixture of anger and sadness. "Everything. Dragging Canoe is right, that if we don't stand our ground here and run those bastards off, we are doomed as a people."

Leotie was at a loss as to how to respond. It seemed as if Yona was even more committed now to Dragging Canoe's ideas than before the attacks. She admitted to herself that she was secretly glad they had been unsuccessful, and she'd hoped her husband would come home ready to consider Nancy's belief that the only path to survival for the

Cherokee was to make peace. But that was obviously not the case. She said no more, just touched his arm lightly and went back to their cabin. Yona did not return that night.

Because the settlers were forewarned, none of the three attacks met with success, but one of the war parties, the one led by old Abram against Fort Caswell, returned to Chota with two hostages, a woman and a young boy. Those who had marched forth determined to wipe out the whites were angry and dispirited at having taken such losses as they did. Their vengeance was turned on the two white hostages. One morning soon after their return, Leotie saw Nancy racing toward her horse.

"Nancy! What's happening?" she cried, running toward her.

"I must get to Toqua now!" was all she said and kicked her horse into a run. Leotie mounted her own horse and raced to catch up with Nancy. "What's happening?" she asked again, breathless.

"Those hostages," Nancy shouted. "They can't kill them in Chota because it's a town of sanctuary, so they've taken them to Toqua. If we don't hurry, they'll kill them there."

They rode their horses as fast as they could to the neighboring village, but they were too late to save the boy. Leotie was horrified to see the blackened corpse of the boy sagging on the post where he'd been burned at the stake. They were about to burn the woman as well when Nancy rode up and jumped from her horse. "No! Let her go," she demanded. "I am your *Gigahyuh*. Show me the respect I deserve." The executioners hesitated. "Give the woman to me, now!" Nancy shouted. "I will have her for my own." Nancy wasn't a tall woman, but she had a regal presence, and she didn't blink when she challenged the warriors. Reluctantly, they untied the terrified woman and led her to Nancy. "Go now," she told the men. "Leave us." Then she turned and took the woman's hand, and the two walked away from the pyre. Leotie heard her say in disgust, "It is this brutality that portrays all Cherokees as ignorant savages."

Leotie was shaken as the three rode back to Chota. Never in their village at Echoe had she witnessed this kind of atrocity or felt the hatred that seemed to pervade these villages now against the white settlers. During the coming days, she overheard conversations between Dragging

Canoe, who had miraculously survived the gunshot wound that tore through both of his thighs, and the English Indian Superintendent Cameron, the one they called Scotchie. She and Nancy learned of the vicious collusion planned between the English and the Indians in an all-out war against the Americans, who, she also learned, had apparently decided to fight for complete independence from England.

Leotie recalled the days of the Regulators and the unhappy outcome of that minor rebellion. Would these new American fighters be able to withstand both the English and their Indian allies? Would they even survive? She thought about Ma and Pa Will. Jeannette and Fergus and little Kate, and she feared even more now for their lives. She'd made her choice to stay with the Cherokees, but a part of her longed to go back to the Catawba Valley, to find a way as Nancy Ward had done to warn her people of the terrible plans about to unfold, plans that threatened all their lives.

CHAPTER TWENTY

Catawba Valley, July 1776

Fiona sat with Kate, Alicia, and Cissy learning how to use the new flax spinning wheel they had brought back from Salisbury. They had grown a small crop of flax on their farm last year, which had been pulled from the ground and laid to rest over the winter in the barn. They'd prepared the dried flax in the springtime, singing as they worked to break the fiber from the stalks, but Fiona had become alarmed when Jeannette seemed to take a special pleasure in the next step, scutching the flax, which meant beating it against a board with a blunt wooden knife.

"Here's to you, Philemon Means," she'd uttered under her breath. "I swear I'll do the same to you if I ever lay eyes on you again." Jeannette beat at the plant fiber so fiercely that Fiona eventually had to grasp the young woman's wrist to stop her.

"That's enough, Jeannette. It's done now."

Jeannette threw down the knife and slammed out the door. "Keep to your woman's work. I'm going to help Pa!"

The other women watched her fly across the yard toward the small blacksmith shop Will had set up away from the house. "She scares me, that one does," Alicia dared to say. "I worry 'bout her, Miss Fiona. She don't seem right in the head these days."

Since that day, Jeannette had shown no interest in the spinning wheel or anything else the women generally did on the homestead. She was busy learning a new craft—gunsmithing.

Today, Fiona put that ugly scene behind her, and as she took her seat by the wheel, she had a warm feeling that her grandmother was there with her in the room, guiding her in the process. She hummed as she spun, feeling deeply contented. But her sense of well-being was broken after only a few moments when a rider galloped into their yard.

"Gordon! Will Gordon! Halloo!"

The women dashed to the front of the cabin to see one of the Davidson boys jump from his horse, his face white and his eyes wild. "What is it, George? What's wrong?" Fiona placed two fingers to the sides of her mouth and let out a loud whistle, a signal they'd used for years to summon the family and helpers from the fields. Will, Fergus, Abe, and Billy came at a run.

The young man literally crumpled into her arms, sobbing. "They's dead, the whole family," he cried.

"Who's dead?" A chill struck through Fiona.

"John. His family. Indians kilt them all."

John Davidson Jr. and his wife, Nancy, had a farm further west of the Gordon homestead. He was one of the five Davidson brothers who had moved earlier to the Catawba Valley, and who had built a fort not far from their homesteads for protection.

After a while, George Davidson regained his composure somewhat and was able to relate what he'd found when he went to visit John. "He was lying dead in his cornfield, and poor Nancy was hung over the fence like a rag doll. They kilt and scalped them all, even the children, and it looks like they took that new little baby and bashed its head against the doorway." He started to cry again, then leaned over the porch rail and vomited.

Fiona motioned to the women to follow her inside. "Alicia, turn on the kettle, and Jeannette, find that liquid corn. This man needs soothing."

Kate looked up at her with her intense green eyes. "Ruth is alive," she said calmly.

Fiona knelt beside her daughter. She'd had inklings that Kate had the Sight. Ruth was one of the Davidson daughters. "How do you know, Kate?" she asked quietly.

The girl just looked at her and shrugged. "Because she wasn't there. She's over yonder visiting her grandma and grandpa."

* * *

The following morning, after an uneasy, almost sleepless night, they were startled by the sound of shouts and thunder of hooves. Will, gun in hand, went to the door and peered out, Fiona right behind him. The riders came up to the farmhouse, led by an elderly woman who sat astride her horse.

"Get ye to Fort McDowell," she cried. Fiona recognized her as Jean Cathey, an early settler whose family had built a fort further to the west. "Them Indians are coming! Everyone must hurry!" Mrs. Cathey dismounted. "They's kilt all them up on Crooked Creek," she said, breathing hard, holding her hand over her heart. "They've kidnapped two of the Burchfield children and three others. Who knows what'll happen to them? Some have taken shelter in our fort, but it isn't sufficient to contain all who need protection. We must all go to Fort McDowell, Charles's place over at Quaker Meadows."

Fiona and the others gave food and water to the riders, who then raced on to warn others of the impending danger.

Will took Fiona by the arm and led her away from the cabin so the others couldn't hear.

"I won't have it happen again," he said, his expression both sad and angry. "I can leave the land, but I will not let these savages kill my family. We will go to McDowell's place. Let us make haste." Almost as an afterthought, he added, "I wonder about Annie and John, and the rest of the Davidsons, the Pattons, that new fellow Carson."

As if in answer, before the day was out, a caravan of refugees, herding cattle and sheep, passed through the Gordon property. Annie McDowell jumped from her wagon and ran to Fiona.

"You must flee! John and Joseph stayed over at Cathey's Fort, but I fear for their lives. Sarah Burchfield's children and three others were snatched by Indians on our way here." She was almost in tears. "Hurry!!!" she implored, then rejoined the group that was hurrying as fast as the livestock would allow along the path by the riverbank.

Fiona took what she could carry in her woolen satchel—her medicinal herbs and the books she'd kept over the years with the secrets of healing, sketches, and other notes. Jeannette, Alicia, Cissy, and even little Kate rushed to collect what food they could carry on their horses.

Fergus, Billy, and Abe helped Will gather their livestock and started them on the trail behind the others. Just as they were about to leave their farm, Fiona, sitting tall in her saddle, turned to look at their beautiful land and the home she loved so dearly. Suddenly, she hopped down from the horse and ran back to the house.

"Fiona! Where are you going?" Will shouted. "We have to run... now!" She heard him but paid him no heed. Instead, she ran to where the two fiddles and Mr. Bentley's Irish flute leaned against a wall alongside the hearth. Nigel Stainton had destroyed the fiddle she'd treasured, the one given her by her Da. She was not about to let these savages take away these that Will had given her, along with the harmony of the good life they had known together.

She was back in a dash, handing one fiddle to Jeannette, another to Alicia. "Hold on tight to those," she ordered. Then she handed the flute to Kate. "I'll teach you to play it soon."

Fiona had fled many times in her life, but never with this sense of terror. She'd always thought her time among the Cherokees would keep her and her family from harm.

But these weren't the Cherokees she knew. These were hateful, cruel murderers.

* * *

In the aftermath of the raids that were carried out by followers of Dragging Canoe, they learned that many houses had been burned to the ground, including the dog trot home of John and Annie McDowell. Scores of settlers had been killed and scalped, including four of the five children who'd been taken from the fleeing refugees. The men had secured the women and children at Fort McDowell, then rode back and were able to relieve those besieged at Fort Cathey. Fiona fully expected their home to be in ashes as well, but apparently the Indians had been repulsed before getting that far to the east of the valley. Their homestead was untouched when they finally returned.

This was but one of numerous attacks by Dragging Canoe's followers that summer, they learned when they received word from Griffith Rutherford that the frontier settlers from South Carolina,

Georgia, and Virginia had suffered similar atrocities.

"Enough!" was the word that seemed to echo throughout the mountains and valleys along the Blue Ridge. "Enough!"

CHAPTER TWENTY-ONE

Davidson's Fort, North Carolina, September 1776

W ill, too, had had enough, and in August, he joined others mustering at Davidson's Fort—McDowell's militia and others from as far away as Surry, Wilkes, and Mecklenburg counties. They gathered in answer to a summons from Brigadier General Griffith Rutherford to join him in a march against the Cherokee Middle Towns to rid the western frontier of the Indian threat once and for all. In July, a small force of Georgians had destroyed Cherokee towns on the Chattahoochee and Tugaloo rivers, and a united plan was made between South and North Carolina and Virginia to move swiftly and mercilessly against all Cherokee towns within those regions.

By this time, word had also come of a daring proclamation made by the Continental Congress, the Declaration of Independence, signed on July 4th in Philadelphia. That conflict was no longer a war to secure their rights as English freemen. It had become a war to create an entirely new country—America. Having officially declared independence from Britain, and with battles already being fought in the northern colonies, the new Americans no longer followed the king's law, and boundaries set by the English were considered no longer valid.

Will considered the expedition they were about to embark upon not so different from the one he'd joined in South Carolina years ago. Although he hated the idea of attacking their towns again and wiping out an entire people, he now firmly believed that the only way to secure the peace he'd been seeking since arriving in America was to shake the bonds of the British. If it meant taking out the Indians, so be it. They'd made their choice.

He also believed if they didn't stop them, the murders, rapes, and kidnappings by those Cherokees following Dragging Canoe would continue. His only fear was that Maura would die as a consequence.

Fergus, now thirteen and as eager as Will had been at that age to prove himself a man, was assigned to guard the homestead with Abe, Billy, and the women, all of whom by now had become proficient with a gun. Will remembered that Margaret and her parents had also been able marksmen, but that hadn't saved their lives. He loathed leaving his family now, but he was compelled to join the Davidsons, McDowells, and other neighbors on this march over the mountains to put a stop to the raids once and for all. Perhaps by taking out these British allies, they would aid the American cause as well.

He wished Cass would return to help protect his family, but they hadn't seen or heard from him since he'd come home with Kate last April. He'd stayed only a few days, then returned to the mountains that called so strongly to him. Will worried that he might be killed or captured by the Indians who were dead set on running the Wataugans and other Overmountain settlers out of their land. Danger from Indians, Tories, and the English lurked everywhere, and Will's determination to protect his family overcame any reluctance of going on this murderous mission.

On September first, nearly twenty-five hundred men began their journey. They rode over the rugged Swannanoa Gap and into the valley below, which Will readily recognized as being one of the places he and Fiona had stopped on their flight out of Cherokee country.

When the marchers passed the place where they had camped, he diverted his horse for a brief period and went in search of a certain sycamore tree. He found it as he remembered, at the river's edge. Still clearly visible carved into the bark were the letters "G.E." Grey Eagle. He grinned, thinking about Fiona's spirited attempt to play that fiddle tune on an Indian flute. He missed her already. Maybe someday, when there was peace, he and Fiona would come back and settle here at Grey Eagle, he thought as he guided his mount back to join the others.

As if he'd read Will's mind, Sam Davidson rode up beside him. "Pretty valley, ain't it?" he said, indicating the land that stretched between two mountain ranges. "Someday I'm going to come back and build me a place around here."

Will laughed. "Let me know when. I might just come with you."

The march lasted just over one month, during which time Rutherford's expedition and the forces of Colonel Andrew Williamson of the South Carolina militia destroyed thirty-six Cherokee villages in the Middle and Valley towns. Theirs was a "scorched earth" campaign, leaving no homes, crops, or livestock in their wake.

The Indians had obviously been warned. Most of the villages were deserted by the time of their arrival, their residents fleeing into the woods and mountains, just as Fiona had been forced to do when he rode with Grant's army years ago.

Will reflected on the irony of that as they headed back toward the Catawba Valley. Then he'd fought for the English. Now he was fighting for the new country, America, against the English and their allies, the Cherokee, who were being paid by the British to hold the western frontier.

Freedom's edge had two sides, he mused. Maybe the Americans were, as Rutherford had told him back in Salisbury, on the edge of freedom. But if their freedom was won in this war, the Cherokees stood to lose theirs. And what about people like Alicia and Billy? Abe and Cissy? They had already lost their freedom. Would the new country take measures to set these people free?

Will later heard that the third expedition of eighteen hundred men led by Virginian Colonel William Christian had successfully marched against the Overhill towns, which they'd found mostly abandoned as well. Word was that some of the tribe from the more southern villages had fled south into British-held west Florida, while those from the Overhill towns had moved westward into Creek and Muscogee territory, toward Chickamauga Creek. He hoped for Maura's sake that she had made it to safety, but his heart was heavy because he believed it was only a matter of time until her tribe, and all the other native peoples, would be destroyed.

* * *

The combined September attacks on all the Cherokee towns achieved their goal—the decimation of the native population. Because the old Cherokee peace chief, Attakulakula, and those of his followers who sought peace lived in Chota, Colonel Christian had spared that village, and it wasn't long before a delegation from there reached the fort on the Holston, begging for peace.

CHAPTER TWENTY-TWO

Chota, April 1777

"**P**ack up, wife. We are leaving these old men to their foolishness," Yona told her after he returned from yet another raiding party led by Dragging Canoe. Leotie was sickened when he rode into the village proudly displaying a scalp he had taken. They had brought with them as captives two young men, sons of the Crockett family, the rest of whom they'd murdered. They had not stopped the negotiations for the proposed treaty they were protesting, but they'd made it clear that the settlers' troubles were far from over. "They think they can still make peace with the white liars." Yona spit on the hard dirt floor. "Each treaty eats away at Cherokee land, and we have resolved to break away."

Dragging Canoe and his followers had fled the onslaught of the American attacks last September, rather than standing and fighting as they had bragged they would. Slowly, many of them had filtered back into Chota over the winter. Now they were agitating against the settlers once again.

"Who has resolved this break away, husband?"

He sneered at her. "Dragging Canoe, of course. He's the only chief left in the tribe with the courage to fight back before it's too late."

"Where are we to go?" she asked, not liking this one bit. In her mind, Dragging Canoe was not only a coward and a murderer, but perhaps also mad.

"To the Chickamauga. South toward the old Muscogee land."

"So, you will be taking the land of others, just like the whites?" she dared. She had become a bit afraid of her husband. Yona had been a different person since the many humiliating defeats suffered by the Cherokee last summer and fall. He was always angry and unsettled. She blamed Dragging Canoe for turning him and others of his people against the elders and traditions that had guided them for centuries. They no longer even listened to their *Giga-hyuh*.

"This is different. Muscogees no longer live there. We share those hunting grounds."

Leotie humphed. Seemed the same to her. She was no stranger to running, but with an infant now to care for, she had no taste for a long and difficult journey on foot or even horseback through the wilderness, chasing the futile dream of the arrogant hothead, Dragging Canoe. At the same time, she wanted her son to know his father before he recklessly got himself killed in one of these raids.

"Please, don't go," she pleaded. "I don't want to go there, and we need you here."

Yona took her face in both hands. Once he'd made this gesture in a loving way. Now, he shook his head, scowling. "You're still white, aren't you?" he muttered angrily. "You are not of our people."

She jerked away from him. "I am of our people," she replied defiantly, "but of those who believe in making peace. Your way will surely lead to exactly what you don't want. The Cherokees and other tribes can't win this war, Yona. The Americans are too strong, too determined. I learned long ago from my Cherokee family that there are times to fight, and times to let go. This is one of those times to let go. Our people must continue to try to live in peace with the new settlers, regardless of their land greed. They have brought our people into a new day, whether we like it or not. Many of our old ways have already disappeared. Those old days are behind us, Yona, but that doesn't mean we can't survive. Unless you and your bloody companions manage to get us all killed."

Yona took her painfully by the arm. "You will go with me. Our son will go with me. I do not wish for him to be brought up by these traitors to our traditions."

Leotie said nothing, thinking he was the one who was a traitor, but again pulled away from his grasp. Suddenly, she was no longer afraid of him, and she was unspeakably angry.

However, he was stronger than she, and she decided this might be one of those times it was better to retreat than fight. Without speaking, she began to gather their belongings. She did not speak to him as they rode away from Chota. She would not speak to him on their journey, she had decided. She did not intend to speak to him ever again.

* * *

"You will get over it," Yona said to her on the third day of their journey to the Chickamauga. "You will see. This will be a better place for us to raise Little Bear."

Leotie remained impassive and rode along in silence, their infant son in his cradleboard strapped to her back.

Yona tried again. "You are being foolish, woman. Talk to me."

Silence.

At last, he gave up and nudged his horse ahead to catch up with Dragging Canoe. Leotie watched his figure disappear into the deep woods and considered for a moment turning her horse around and heading back to Chota. But three days had passed, and she was unsure whether she could make her way alone. Resolutely, she stayed the course.

They had ridden through a few of the villages that had been destroyed by Colonel Christian and his troops. Homeless survivors from Big Island Town, Settico, Tellico, and Chilhowee joined the flight of the dispossessed, being dispirited and uninterested in rebuilding their ravaged towns. Leotie was sickened and saddened by the devastation, and she knew had she and her mother and brother returned to Echoe instead of moving east with Will Gordon, they would have found their homes destroyed in like manner.

When would the madness end? As Maura, she had lived with the whites and understood their desire for land and freedom. As Leotie, she'd lived with the Indians, and she understood as well, their desire to hold onto their land and traditions. What she didn't understand was her place among either.

Her mind grew numb with these troublesome thoughts, and she withdrew even from the company of the other women who were moving to Chickamauga. Yona rode alongside her for most of the journey, taking Little Bear from her when they stopped to rest. He had ceased trying to talk with her, and they communicated in silence for the care of the child.

She did not find their new home to be a better place than Chota. It was a smattering of rude cabins constructed around the commissary of John McDonald, one of the Englishmen who was providing the renegade Cherokees, who were now calling themselves "Chickamoogees," with supplies and ammunition.

She heard a cheer go up when they arrived, and many hurried to gather around Dragging Canoe, who obviously was a hero in their eyes. It wasn't long before the brash young warrior had gathered a large following, and Leotie heard him immediately begin to incite them to attack white settlers.

Yona and others hastily constructed a modest cabin for Leotie and Little Bear, but he no longer slept with her. In fact, she was never sure of his whereabouts. He dutifully provided meat and fish. Any other food she foraged from the forest. For all intents and purposes, their marriage was over.

It was in the autumn, that time of great change, when the leaves turned to brilliant reds and golds, that Leotie made up her mind to leave. She knew she could not abide these Cherokee traitors much longer. Yona was right—she was not of these people, these murderers. She didn't know how or when she would go, but she began a vision quest to guide her. She had not been trained by Nanyeh or Quella, not even her mother, in focusing on her inner spirit and bringing forth visions of what might be, but she began trying to see if she had inherited any of her grandmother's mystical powers. Each night as she lay down to sleep, she brought a vision of her brother, Cass, into her mind. Sometimes she saw him on his horse, riding toward her. At other times, he just appeared on foot out of the woods. She didn't know if there was power in these visions, but they gave her comfort...and hope. Somehow, she felt in her heart, he would hear her and come to take her home.

CHAPTER TWENTY-THREE

Washington County, North Carolina, Spring 1779

Cass Gordon lived alone in a small cabin he kept near Sycamore Shoals when he wasn't out hunting or trapping. He was a tall, muscular young man of twenty-six, and more than one young woman in the settlement had her eye on him. Cass enjoyed the company of women but had managed so far to remain unencumbered by wife or family. It was at times like the present, he thought, saddling his horse and packing his gear, that it was best he was still a single man. He was riding out today with Colonel Evan Shelby, and their target was the Chickamogees.

Dragging Canoe and his conspirators had continued their savage attacks on those living on the outer edges of the frontier. Cass had been especially horrified at the murders of old David Crockett and his family at the time of the signing of the Treaty of Great Island a couple of years back. Two of his boys had been spared, but kidnapped. Cass didn't want to think about what kind of torture the bloodthirsty Indians had likely inflicted on them.

In January, Virginia Governor Patrick Henry had ordered Shelby to gather at least three hundred men in the district to go at once to destroy the five towns that had been built by the Chickamauga Cherokees, and with them, Dragging Canoe and his followers. Cass volunteered, out of loyalty to the American cause, but also because he still held out a flicker of hope that one day, he might find Maura. He had spoken with Nancy Ward, who continued to maintain her friendship with many of the white settlers, and he'd learned that his sister had left Chota with her husband who'd followed Dragging Canoe to Chickamauga Creek. Even if he found her, he wondered what she would be like. Had she swallowed the poison offered by Dragging Canoe, his venomous hatred for all whites? Another thought had chilled him. Maura was half white. Would that crazy Indian have harmed her because of that?

He was with six hundred militia men from North Carolina and Virginia as they headed toward Chickamauga Creek, traveling by dugout canoe down the Tanase River, hoping to engage Dragging Canoe and his band of murderers and wipe them out for good. But when they arrived, approaching the first village on foot hoping the element of surprise would be in their favor, they were the ones surprised.

The warriors were away fighting on behalf of the British on the Georgia and South Carolina borders. Only women, children, and the elderly remained. They took the village without a shot being fired.

And then he saw her, a small woman standing stiffly erect outside a cabin, a little boy by her side. A mixture of relief and apprehension washed over him as he went over to her.

"Maura?"

She looked at him, tears shining in her eyes. "Cass. I knew you would come. Please, take me home."

* * *

He had come, just as she had envisioned. He had stepped out of the forest as if by magic.

He had come to take her out of this place, to take her home.

Maura did not look back as they began the long journey to Cass's place, nor did she pity those who remained, despite knowing they would once again be homeless and hungry. It had been their choice to come with Dragging Canoe. It was never hers.

Behind them, she later learned, Shelby's men burned eleven towns, destroyed McDonald's commissary, and confiscated his stash of winter peltries along with the ammunition stores provided by the British. Twenty thousand bushels of corn were taken from the Indians.

They would indeed go hungry now.

At first, she and Cass spoke little on their journey together back to Sycamore Shoals. She had withheld her speech for so long, it was difficult for her to open up again. Gradually, speaking became easier for her, and she began to ask questions. "How is our family, Cass? Have you been to see them lately?"

Cass told her he had managed his way down the mountain from

time to time, visiting his family and friends who now were firmly settled in the Catawba Valley. "They are doing well, or as well as can be expected," he said. "There is the war with the English to consider, and the ongoing fight with the Indians. Pa Will and Fergus have joined Colonel McDowell's militia."

"Fergus! Is he old enough?"

Cass laughed. "You've been away for a while, and kids grow up. He's sixteen now and full of himself wanting to be a man."

As they walked, Cass carried Little Bear, who was barely two years old, most of the way, and questioned Maura in return about the renegade Indians in general, and Yona in particular.

"Do you think he will come after you?" he asked. Maura was silent for a long while, and Cass added, "I'm just wondering if the time could come when I might have to kill my sister's husband."

"He is no longer my husband. We are no longer married. I divorced him...you know...Indian style." And at that, they both laughed, knowing it was far easier for Indian women to regain their independence than their white sisters. "As far as killing him," she paused, unsure of how she felt about that. "I'd rather you didn't, of course, because he's Little Bear's father, but if that's what it takes to defeat Dragging Canoe, then, yes, you must," she added, and their laughter ceased.

Maura begged Cass to take them to Chota before continuing to Sycamore Shoals. "I must see Nancy once again," she pleaded when he said he didn't want to go there. "I must let her know I am alive and moving back among the settlers."

Chota was a shadow of its former glory despite having been spared by Colonel Christian's army a couple of years back. Many Indians had deserted and left for the new Chickamauga settlements to the south, others on to new ground further west. But Nancy Ward was among those who remained. Maura saw her old friend and dashed into Nancy's arms, and her fierce embrace was returned. Both women wept.

They stayed the night with Nancy and her children, her husband Bryan having returned to his white wife in Virginia. The following morning, Nancy gave them two horses for the remainder of their journey, for which Cass was grateful. It had been a good tactical idea to take the water route to take the Chickamaugas by surprise, but it had been a long walk back. Nancy also gave Maura a letter of introduction to her friends in the Watauga settlements, along with a cow that had been born from one of those Mrs. Bean had given to her after Nancy had saved her from burning at the stake.

The two women bade a tearful farewell. Maura was silent for most of the rest of trip, not because she didn't want to talk to her brother, but rather because it was difficult over the tightness in her throat. She wondered if she would ever see Nancy again. Wondered if Nancy, too, would eventually become a victim of Dragging Canoe's madness.

They reached Cass's cabin late on a warm, sunny afternoon a few days later. "I didn't remember how beautiful this place was," Maura murmured, gazing up at the sunshine sifting through the fresh green leaves of the sycamores that lined the banks of the river. They had passed by here, or a place very much like it, when she'd been kidnapped by Yona.

Dismounting, she took Little Bear from his seat on the saddle in front of her brother. The child had made most of the journey from Chota riding with Cass. He'd traveled without much fuss, and Cass had kindly stopped frequently to let him run and play. "Thanks for carrying him with you," she said.

"He's a good boy," Cass said, tousling his nephew's dark black hair.

"Yes, he is, and I want him to grow up to be a good man," Maura replied. She settled Little Bear and herself into the cabin after Cass insisted he could make do outside since it was now summer. That evening, after Cass had resupplied his provisions and made supper for the three of them, Maura sat by the fire they'd built outside of his cabin. It was a pleasant early summer evening, fireflies just beginning to flicker as the late sun set.

For the first time since being kidnapped by Yona, Maura found herself able to relax and laugh again. She could now see that even in the early years of their marriage, when she'd been happy with him, there had been an undercurrent of tension she hadn't recognized. She suddenly realized she'd never really trusted him. After all, he'd been her captor first, husband second, and it hadn't been her choice to marry him. "What a mistake I have made," she said soberly. "I should have come back with you that day you came and took Kate home."

They sat in silence, watching Little Bear running around in the grass, chasing fireflies.

"That can't be undone, Maura," Cass said gently. "Do you want me to take you home now?"

"I'm not sure. When I think of going back to Ma and Pa Will, it somehow doesn't seem right. I'm a half-breed, and my son is even more Indian than I. Look at him, that hair, that skin. He'll never be able to disguise his Indian blood even if he wanted to." She drew in a deep breath and let it out slowly. "I remember how I was treated by some of the whites." She paused, then added, "I don't want that for my son." She felt her lips tremble, and she swallowed hard. "I don't know where home is anymore, Cass."

He took her hand and squeezed it. "I know the feeling. It took me a long time, and a lesson from old Quella, to make me understand that I am one with the whites." She was astonished when he told her of that night in Hiram Greenlee's cabin when Quella had spoken to Onacona in the spirit world.

"I miss him," she said, looking up at the sky where stars were just beginning to show themselves. "Onacona was my father. Much as I came to love Will, it wasn't the same."

Cass didn't reply for a long while, and when he spoke, his voice was low and taut. "I have had two fathers," he said. "Onacona and Will. Neither is my real father. I wonder if I'll ever learn who it was who sired me, and why Ma ran away from him."

A spark of a memory crossed Maura's mind. "I think he was English," she said. "I overheard her speaking with Nanyeh once, the first time we ran away into the woods when the English soldiers came. I was very young, but it seems to me she was worried a man might be coming with the soldiers, someone she didn't want to know where she was." She paused, considering her next words carefully. "Being a woman, I know what can happen if a man who is stronger than you takes you." She was embarrassed but managed to continue. "You know what I mean by that."

Cass nodded. "I do. And I've long thought I might be the son of a man who raped Ma."

There it was, out in the open, what neither had been willing to look at. Rape.

"If that is so," Maura said, "it is no wonder she's never wanted to talk about it. It has never happened to me, but only because Yona was determined I was to marry him. Other captive women haven't been so fortunate, if you can call it that."

Little Bear was growing weary and came to sit on Maura's lap. She ran her fingers through his thick black hair. "And now there is this one, who with any luck will never know his father either." She broached a subject that she'd been wrestling with in her mind during the whole trip. "Cass, I want him to grow up knowing the white man's ways. It will be difficult, but it must be. That is our future. Yona and Dragging Canoe and all those others are fighting a losing battle. We will soon all be Americans. Little Bear must learn how to live in that world."

She paused again. "A good start would be to give him a white man's name. He won't make it as Little Bear."

Maura put Little Bear to bed on his blanket inside the cabin, then returned to sit by the fire with Cass. "About that white man's name. What could we call him?"

Cass thought a moment. "Do you want to name him after someone, like Will maybe?"

"No. I want him to be his own person. Unless, of course, he's named after somebody really important."

"How about George, like George Washington. He's really important."

"Isn't George also the king of England, who's causing all these troubles?"

"Good point," Cass said. He scratched his head. "Well, then, how about something from the Bible? Like Joseph or John?"

But Maura shook her head. "Too many Josephs already. And

Johns. Besides, I don't think I want a Biblical name. If I'm going to name him after someone, I want it to be a gentleman, a man who is educated and respected. A man from our time who might serve as a model for him when he grows up."

Cass sighed. He was silent so long Maura thought maybe he'd gone to sleep. Then suddenly, he sat up straight and said, "I've got it! I've got the perfect name! A gentleman's name, for sure!"

Chapter Twenty-Four

Catawba Valley, Summer 1779

Fiona awoke from a vivid dream, in which she'd seen her family reunited, with Cass and Maura at home around the family table. Much as she wished it to be, she couldn't quite believe it, even though dreams were part of her Sight. Maura, she feared, was gone to them forever.

And yet...her dreams rarely failed her.

She arose and dressed for the day, wondering what it would bring. Each day was filled with uncertainty. The unrest among the settlers was palpable even when words went unspoken.

Not only did they have the Indians to fear, now some of their neighbors were siding with the English, and it was hard to know who to trust. Tories. Spies. It took Fiona's strength of will to look some of them in the eye at community gatherings, knowing they would turn against her family if push came to shove and the English arrived at their doorstep.

After breakfast, Fiona and Alicia headed for the vegetable garden that was beginning to bear an abundant summer crop. Billy worked alongside Will in the fields while Abe tended the cattle and other livestock. Cissy had recently given birth to her first child, Ben, who now rocked in the cradle that had held Fergus and Kate. Fergus, eager to fight with the American patriots, was off with Charles McDowell's militia, much to Fiona's distress.

Oddly, Jeannette had taken over the smithy and had learned how to make weapons as well as tools and horseshoes, also to Fiona's distress. She wasn't sure what to make of Jeannette these days. Her stepdaughter had taken to dressing like a man, sewing her skirts together in the center, then cutting them to make pantaloons and tucking them into knee-high boots. Jeannette's grief, and her anger, had never been satiated, and until she came out of it, Fiona chose to let her be. Kate, now seven, was old enough to help Cissy in the kitchen and was becoming adept at making pies.

Fiona was worried about Fergus and the American war, which apparently was going badly. Some of the local boys had signed up with other North Carolina militia and had fought in battles in the northern colonies. They returned with stories of glory and defeat. Mostly defeat, it had seemed of late.

Will was also part of McDowell's militia but riding out only as needed. With the war at a stalemate in the north, the British had shifted their attention to the southern colonies, believing they had a great deal of Tory support there. Thinking of certain neighbors, Fiona knew this could be true. She also remembered Philemon Means and that drunken doctor and wondered where those two Tories were now. Cass had managed a few visits, each time bringing news of the Overmountain people, none of it very good either. The renegade Cherokees continued to attack white settlers, and white settlers continued to encroach on Indian lands. It was like a tidal surge that couldn't be halted, whether it was right or wrong.

"Cass is coming again," Kate shouted, running to Fiona and breaking into her thoughts. Fiona stood and wiped her brow with the back of her hand, her heart leaping. "Is he here?" she asked, looking around.

"No. But he'll be here tomorrow. And he's bringing Maura."

Fiona closed her eyes and was finally able to believe it. Her dreams rarely failed her. She knelt so she was eye-level with her small daughter. She looked into those piercing green eyes.

"Maura? Are you sure?" She had experienced enough of Kate's foresight to trust it. It was as if her daughter was the re-embodiment of her Granny.

Kate grinned. "I'm sure. And there's another coming with them."

Her heart surging with joy, Fiona jumped to her feet. "We must make ready!" she cried.

"Alicia! Come!" She and Kate ran hand in hand toward the kitchen shack behind the main cabin, Alicia at their heels. Their homestead had grown, as had their dwellings, and they had hitherto escaped the

Indians' destruction. The cabin now had a new kitchen shack out back, for more space as well as fire safety. The Africans had cabins of their own. There was a barn for the animals, including several horses. The fields bore flax and had produced acres of corn for several years now, and Will had taught Fergus the art of making the "liquid corn" he'd learned from the first Fergus: Fergus McKinney. Even the apple and peach trees were maturing and bearing fruit. In all, their lives had prospered in the Catawba Valley.

If only this war business would end. If only the Indians would let them be. If only...

The following day, Kate's prediction came true. It was a Sunday, and the family gathered on the front lawn beneath the large shade tree. A big dinner was waiting, and everyone was pensive and anxious to see if Kate was right or if she'd just been making it up to get attention.

But they all knew of the little girl's strange abilities to see the future.

About an hour past midday, Kate, who'd climbed the big tree to get a better lookout, cried out, "Here they come!"

Almost as one, the group rose and looked across the field to where Kate was pointing. At first, Fiona saw nothing, and then slowly the apparition appeared, turning her dream into a reality. Two horses approached, one ridden by a tall red-headed man, the other by a dark-haired young woman. And in front of the man rode a very small boy.

Fiona fought tears. She ran like the wind toward the approaching figures, and Maura leapt from her horse as soon as she saw her mother. They came together in a crash of happiness. "Oh, my daughter, my Maura. I thought never to see you again."

They held one another until both were nearly out of breath and out of tears. Finally, they parted to see the rest of the family surrounding them, waiting their turns to welcome her home.

Maura turned to each with a warm embrace, and when she reached Will, she put her head against his chest and held him close. "Pa, I have missed you so much."

Fiona saw it was Will's turn to cry. Maura had always called him 'Pa Will,' keeping him in a way at arm's length as her father. Now, he was simply 'Pa.'"

In fact, they were all in tears when Cass said, "Hey, everybody, there's someone else here to welcome."

They turned to him, as if he had just ridden up, and Fiona saw the little boy squirming in his arms. "This is our new boy, Maura's son," Cass said, holding the child above his head. "Say hello to Thomas Jefferson!"

* * *

Their reunion was short-lived and shadowed by the continuing absence of Fergus. Maura was deeply distraught at the thought that her little brother could be in the line of British fire.

She'd heard all the talk about the wars, both with the Indians and the British. She thought and thought about what she could do, what she should do, to help the Americans win. As each day passed, she grew restless, and then an idea came to her. She approached Cass, who was preparing to return to Watauga.

"Take me with you," she said resolutely. "I made friends while I was there earlier, and there's one in particular I would like to assist. Her name is Mary Patton."

Jeannette overheard their conversation. "I've heard of Mary Patton," she said, dusting her hands on her pantaloons. "She's the one making black powder up yonder, isn't she?"

Cass laughed. "You're talking about Powder Mary, up on Powder Branch. She learnt powder making from her Da back in Pennsylvania before she and John up and moved to the Overmountain place." He turned to Maura. "Why on earth would you want to assist Mary Patton? Making black powder is a nasty business."

"I know," Maura replied in her quiet way. "She showed me how she does it." She shrugged. "Not much different from making biscuit dough, seems to me."

Cass snorted. "Biscuit dough made out of manure!"

But Maura just shrugged, unmoved. There were wars going on. Black powder would be needed, and she liked Mary. It seemed helping to make black powder was something she could contribute. Yes, it was a nasty business. But if Mary could do it, so could she.

"I want to go too," Jeannette said suddenly. "I'm a good blacksmith. I make good guns. Maybe I could make good black powder too."

Cass looked at her in astonishment. "What? Why?"

Jeannette pulled her long hair behind her neck and bound it with twine. "Because I'm a woman, I can't go off with the militia like Fergus. I want to do something to win this war and finally defeat the Indians, too. Maura's got the right idea." Then she laughed. "I never thought of making black powder as women's work, though."

"Ma's not going to like this one bit," Cass said, shaking his head.

And she didn't. Neither did Will. But when the women explained their reasons, the parents could find little argument. The war had moved to the south and was getting closer to them every day. Everybody was needed in some capacity.

"Leave T.J. with us," Fiona implored, using the boy's nickname. "He will be safe here."

Maura turned a sad eye to her mother. "Will he, Ma? Really? I never felt too safe around white people, except those up yonder where Cass lives. There's lots of families there with Indian children, mostly white men who've married Cherokee women. T.J. will grow up learning the ways of the whites without being taunted about his being Indian. And maybe, someday," she added ruefully, "I might be able to see my friend Nancy again, when all this fighting is behind us."

"If we're still alive," Jeannette muttered.

CHAPTER TWENTY-FIVE

Catawba Valley, June 1780

"Those bloody butchers!" Will cried out when his son Fergus finally made his way back to the farm after serving under American Colonel Abraham Buford at the battle of Waxhaws in South Carolina. According to Fergus, who arrived muddy, scratched, and visibly shaken, Buford had signaled surrender when their forces were overcome, but British Colonel Banastre Tarleton ignored the white flag and allowed his soldiers to murder the Americans, giving no quarter to those who were unable to escape.

Will was scarcely able to control his emotions as his son related the horrors endured by the American soldiers. "They bayonetted all the bodies, Pa," Fergus said, his face pale and anguished. "Just speared them, dead 'uns and live 'uns, tossing bodies about using their bayonets like they was hayforks."

Fergus's words conjured the horror of that cold wet day upon Culloden Moor when Will lost his Da and the rest of his clan to Cumberland, "the butcher." He took Fergus in his arms and held him tight. Somehow, Providence had kept his boy safe from the British butchers. But for how long?

These times were difficult and complex. And dangerous. Since Will had ridden out on Rutherford's expedition nearly four years ago, hoping and expecting that to be the end of the Indian troubles, raids had only worsened. Those following Dragging Canoe, empowered by the British, had continued to attack and murder settlers throughout the southern frontier. The War for Independence had now moved to the south, and the British general Cornwallis had recently taken Charlestown. Even some of their neighbors, people they'd called friends, were proving to be Tories and turning on those with Whig sympathies.

Fiona sat opposite them at their table, pretending not to listen as she stitched on a quilt square, but Will saw her hands shaking, and her head was bowed. "Let's take a walk, son," he said and led young Fergus out of her earshot. "You were eager to go fighting. What do you think about it now?"

Fergus inhaled deeply and looked up at the sky. "I've not been in a lot of battles, Pa, but that one was terrible, as I now imagine most are. But from what I hear, it's come down to them or us. The Tories are doing frightful things to the locals, Pa, killing 'em, burning farms, giving help to the Brits. If we don't kill 'em and the Brits, they'll hang us all." He looked at his father. "I'd rather fight and die than be like them."

Will was torn. He knew Fiona and Kate needed him, but now that Cass, Maura, and Jeannette were living in the Overmountain settlements, all of them dedicated to the cause of freedom, he felt he should join Fergus and McDowell. "When are you going back to your unit?" he asked Fergus.

"Tomorrow. I only came to let you know I am alive, and to give you the warning from Colonel McDowell. Soon them Brits will be on our doorstep."

* * *

The next day, after giving close instructions to Billy and Abe, talking quietly to Fiona to try to calm her fears and her sorrow, and loading some supplies to aid McDowell's militia, Will set out with Fergus, headed for Quaker Meadows. On the way, they were joined by Jake and Joe Paterson. George and his son-in-law David remained to protect their large family and to guard the mill and keep it running.

It wasn't long before McDowell's men were called upon. "Heard from Rutherford there's a Tory bunch gathering over at Ramsour's Mill," Charles McDowell told his assembled fighters.

Griffith Rutherford was in Charlotte, keeping a close eye on the activities of Lord Rawdon and his troops, Cornwallis's men at Camden, in South Carolina. This gathering of Tories was troubling for more reasons than their support of Rawdon. It was a gathering of fellow North Carolinians, traitors to the American cause, and traitors to their neighbors, at least in Rutherford's eyes. "He's sent Colonel Locke and Major Wilson over to put them down," McDowell continued, "and we're to catch up with them at Clark's Creek over in Lincoln County."

Will and Fergus joined the other riders on a night journey along a dark, winding road through heavy woods, leading the infantry toward Ramsour's Mill. Suddenly a band of riders appeared out of the darkness, and Will shouldered his rifle. But Locke ordered them to hold fire.

"Stand and identify yourselves," he called out into the darkness.

"Name's Reep," one of the men shouted back. "I live around here. Come to warn you 'bout the Tory force camped nearby." The farmer told Locke and Wilson that the Tories were well-positioned, camped on a ridge about three hundred yards east of the mill. Worse, they had a two-hundred-yard field of fire down to the roadway.

The firefight started not long after, when riders from another North Carolina militia encountered a Tory picket force and began firing, which warned the Tories of the impending attack, robbing Locke of the surprise he'd hoped for.

"This is going to be rough," Will warned Fergus as they loaded their rifles and fired at the oncoming Tories. "Go for the ones with the pine needles in their caps. And take that off," he ordered his son, pointing to the paper tag that was pinned to his lapel, identifying him as a Whig.

"Makes a good target."

The fighters on both sides were amateurs. After firing into each other's ranks at near point-blank range, not having time to reload, and not having bayonets, they fell on one another using gun butts, knives, rocks, and fists. Will felt a blow to his head and fell to the ground, only semi-conscious. He lay there, stunned, flashing back to that muddy field of Culloden Moor.

Where was Pa? Where was Duncan? And then he remembered he was not on Culloden Moor but rather on a hillside in North Carolina.

Where was Fergus?

He staggered to his feet, looking around desperately for his son. Fergus emerged from the smoke and dust, dirty and bruised, but smiling. He helped his father to his feet. The fighting subsided as the Tory line fell back to the crest of the ridge, retreating down the slope to an encampment of other British sympathizers. The Whig fighters backed away as well and made camp for the night.

"I saw him, Pa," Fergus said as they ate the dried meat and corn bread that was available from McDowell's commissary rations.

"Saw who?"

"Philemon Means. The one that married Jeannette, then up and left her."

Will's blood froze. "Was he alive when you saw him?"

"He was. Don't know if he is now or not. I'd like to have shot him myself but didn't have no more bullets."

"If I ever find him, I'll do the job myself," Will muttered, and meant it.

The following morning, they learned that the British leaders who had started the fight had fled back to Rawdon's force at Camden, and most of the Tories had disbanded and headed for their homes. Will and Fergus joined others—family and friends of both sides from neighboring communities—to bury the dead, all victims of this tragic partisan civil war. They worked alongside to dig a trench on the hillside, and in it they buried fifty-six bodies, Tories and Whigs alike. McDowell's militia regrouped and rode back to the Catawba Valley in sober silence.

* * *

Fiona rushed to Will and Fergus as they returned to the farmhouse and hugged them both soundly. "Thank God you are alive," she said, her voice husky with relief.

Fergus took the horses to the river's edge to drink, Abe and Billy running to him. Will sank onto the wooden bench on the front porch, fatigue overtaking him. Fiona sat on a stool opposite and signaled for him to raise one foot and then the other to her knee. She gently pulled off his boots. His feet hurt, and he was certain they didn't smell so good, but Fiona seemed not to mind. Only when he felt the cool air on his skin did he realize the pain that throbbed in his big toe that had been broken so long ago.

As if she read his mind, she asked, "Does it hurt?" Tenderly she stroked the toe which still remained at an unnatural angle.

"Aye, wife," he said, trying to laugh. He had bouts from time to time when his toe became inflamed, but he had hidden his pain from her. Or so he thought, but each time, without being asked, she brought him a tonic of apple cider vinegar, claiming it would be good for his digestion. Each time, it cured his toe.

Fiona asked Kate to bring her father a bucket of water from the river. It was cold but felt delicious against the hot summer air. When he'd bathed and dried his feet, Fiona appeared with a cup. "Here, drink this. It'll feel better."

Sure enough. Apple cider vinegar.

And sure enough, his aching toe felt better.

CHAPTER TWENTY-SIX

Catawba Valley, September 1780

All summer, Will, Fergus, and many of their neighbors had ridden with Colonel McDowell, skirmishing with roaming bands of Tories who now seemed to pose the most immediate threat to the safety and security of the settlers. The bigger peril, the British army, had become even more threatening after the devastating defeat of American General Horatio Gates at the recent battle of Camden. Will had been distraught to learn that his old friend and commander, Griffith Rutherford, had been taken prisoner there.

Now, Cornwallis's new Inspector of Militia Major Patrick Ferguson had been turned loose to recruit all Tories and conquer the outlying North and South Carolina frontier. As he and his forces moved north, many former patriots surrendered to his demand that they sign a loyalty oath to the king, some on threat of hanging or having their farms and homes burned to the ground.

Fiona had sent Abe up to Watauga to see if he could fetch more black powder and ammunition from Mary Patton's mill. With Billy the only man left on the farm, the women prepared to fight in case the Tories came to call. It might not be a fight they could win, but she was determined not to turn against the Americans, her friends and neighbors, and most especially, her family, no matter what.

As did many of their neighbors, they fortified their place as much as possible. They dug a ditch around the cabins and barns and drained river water into it, hoping it would surprise any intruders and disable their horses if they fell into the unexpected hole. Inside the circle of the ditch they constructed an abatis of fallen trees as a second line of defense. Then they cleared the land on both sides of grass and debris that might catch fire. With these precautions in place, if either the Tories or Ferguson's raiders approached, there would be no question that Fiona and her family were Whigs.

But to her surprise, their first visitors were not Tories, nor Ferguson's men, but her own neighbors, Hunting John McDowell and his son, Joseph, leading the way. They arrived in broad daylight, saw the ditch and the abatis, and hailed Fiona from the perimeter. She showed them the one entrance they'd left open to give them access to their fields. "Glad to see you forting up here," the older McDowell said as he dismounted and stepped onto her porch." He took off his old felt hat, then shook her hand and looked around. "I hear Will and Fergus was with McDowell's bunch at Allen's Mountain after Ferguson routed them at Cane Creek."

This was all news to Fiona. She never knew where they were going, or what battles they were fighting, and the not-knowing was killing her. "Are they...did they..." She couldn't finish her question, but McDowell grinned.

"I think they gave those redcoats a run for their money, but they had to back off. But funny thing happened up there at the mountain. Them Brits left their horses tied to trees at the base of the mountain, too steep for 'em to climb. Our boys found 'em and made off with 'em as they escaped. Guess those redcoats had to walk back to Gilbert Town."

"Gilbert Town!" Fiona exclaimed. "That's pretty close."

"Ferguson's encamped there and raiding around here, recruiting Tories, and stealing cattle and provisions. That's why we've come to see you."

Fiona invited them all inside and offered them spring water. "We aren't about to give up our beeves and hogs to those thieving bastards... uh, sorry, let that slip," the old longhunter said.

"I'm not offended by strong language describing these scoundrels," she assured him, anxious to hear his plan. "Please go on."

He explained that many of the settlers further west in the Catawba Valley had convened and decided to take what cattle and other livestock they could and hide them away in the deep coves of the Blue Ridge mountains, leaving only diminished herds for the British to appropriate.

"We've assigned three of our own to take the oath and ask for protection to throw 'em off what we're doing."

Fiona frowned. "Who would do such a thing?" she asked, thinking it sounded more like a betrayal.

"John Carson, and Benjamin and William Davidson."

Fiona was astounded, as she knew these men well enough to know that not one of them had a Tory breath in their body. She let out a heavy sigh and shook her head, not completely understanding how this would help the American cause.

McDowell reached across the table and took her hand. "It's okay. Don't worry. We have a plan. Now, we came to see if you'd like us to drive your stock with the rest into the mountains. If we don't, Ferguson's sure to get his hands on them."

Fiona looked at Alicia, who was standing by the stove with wide, frightened eyes. Kate started to cry, and Fiona summoned her. "Don't be afraid," she said to her daughter. "These are our friends. They've come to help us." She fervently hoped that to be true. Her instincts told her to trust them, but trust was hard to come by these days.

Before she agreed, she said, "You said Will and Fergus were with McDowell at Allen's Mountain. Do you know where they are now?"

"McDowell is making haste to get beyond the mountain ridges, so I reckon your boys are with him. Seems Ferguson has taken it all personal that he hasn't been able to capture or kill the colonel." Hunting John gave a low chuckle at this. "Old Charlie may seem slow to some, but he's got a smart head. I doubt Ferguson will ever nab him."

Fiona was relieved to know that Will and Fergus had been seen alive only a short time ago, and she understood their loyalty to Charles McDowell. But a part of her wanted desperately for her menfolk to come back and defend their homestead.

She agreed to turn over most of her herd to Hunting John and his men, leaving only a milk cow and her calf to sacrifice to the British major if necessary. There were a few chickens and two hogs left on the farm when they herded the rest away, heading for the mountains.

* * *

It wasn't long before Major Ferguson himself paid a visit to many of the farms in the Catawba Valley, and the Gordon's place didn't escape his careful search for provisions. Hunting John had told her that keeping their army fed was becoming a major problem for the British the further they pushed toward the mountains. "Their supplies come by sea, through Charlestown and Savannah," he explained. "They're pretty much used up by the time their soldiers get halfway through South Carolina. And now they're pushing even further into North Carolina."

Fiona saw the riders approaching, and her stomach lurched. She picked up her hunting rifle, having loaded it after McDowell left, wanting to be prepared. "Stay inside," she told Kate and the others.

"Billy's out in the barn," Alicia wailed.

"I hope he has the good sense to stay there," Fiona replied, a little too sharply. Her nerves were on edge, but she managed a small smile at her long time African friend. "I'm sure he does," she added. Then she straightened her back and stepped out onto the porch, closing the door firmly behind her.

A small band of men rode with Ferguson, already driving a herd of cattle they had purloined. But only the major and three other men found their way across the ditch and fallen trees.

She recognized the turncoats immediately, and she knew how they had so easily picked their way through her defenses. The Davidsons had built fortifications around their homes before construction of what was known in the valley as Davidson's Fort. They would understand that even a strong abatis must have an entry point if the owners wanted to work in their fields outside the barricade.

But were they turncoats? McDowell had said they were part of a plan, but they looked mighty friendly with the major. If they threatened her family and her farm in any way, she would shoot first and ask questions later. It crossed her mind to shoot the major right now and save everyone a lot of trouble, but she was no murderer. Besides, there would be witnesses, and she would hang, she considered with dark humor. Instead, she stood stock still and watched them approach.

Ferguson was not a big man. He was slender, with a round face and delicate features. But from the way he carried himself, and of course the uniform and insignia he wore, there was no doubt this was the man Cornwallis had sent to conquer the wayward backcountry Americans.

She noted he held the reins in his left hand, that his right arm appeared to be disabled.

"Good afternoon, madam," he said, giving her a charming smile. "I bring you greetings from the King of England."

"I do not know him," she replied coldly. "Why would he want to greet me?" She would not succumb to this man's obvious charm. She looked at John Carson, giving him an unspoken question—are you really with this man? He returned her gaze, and she thought she saw an almost imperceptible turn of his head. Did that mean no, he wasn't, or don't say anything to give him away? Or did she just imagine it?

"He asks that you come to know him better," the major went on, undaunted. "I have come to suggest, and strongly, that you and your family have a change of mind and join us as Tories to defeat this illegal insurrection."

"I know why you've come, Major Ferguson," she addressed him sternly, as if she was his school marm. "You've come for my cattle and swine, and anything else you can get your hands on to feed men who are out to kill me and my family."

He laughed good-naturedly, but the humor didn't reach his eyes. "That too. But you might want to rethink taking the oath, as these three, your good neighbors have done."

She wanted to scream at him that they'd done no such thing, at least not honestly, but managed to keep her mouth shut. "My pitiful herd is out yonder, easy pickings for your pirates. I'll have my man bring the swine out to you. Now, major, and you three," she gave them what she hoped was a terrible scowl, "get off my land." She held her breath, hoping they would comply, but then John Carson spoke up.

"How many cattle do you have here?" he asked her.

"Only that old milk cow and her calf. The one that feeds our children," she added pointedly. "And two hogs, too young to butcher to any effect."

Carson turned to Ferguson. "Would be a pity to take such a meager prize, major. Especially a milk cow that supplies food for this woman's family."

Ferguson turned to him, frowning. "Getting soft on your neighbors, Carson?"

"Not at all, sir. But time is of the essence, if I understand you correctly. It will take time to gather and bring these few animals into your custody. Instead, I suggest we ride to where I know of a much larger herd of beeves that can provide a far greater harvest for your endeavor."

Ferguson considered this a moment, then turned and tipped his hat at Fiona. "Then we will leave you in peace, madam, at least for now." Giving his attention once again to John Carson and the Davidsons, he added, "You'd better be giving me good advice. I reserve a certain, may I say, unpleasant, punishment for those who lie to me."

Two days later, Abe returned from his Overmountain journey, and to Fiona's great relief and delight, Will was with him. But where was Fergus? Her stomach knotted. She saw Will was limping as he walked toward her. Had he been shot?

But he had not. It was that toe again, and it was getting worse. "I even tried the apple cider trick," he told her. "Didn't work this time. Must be your magic formula," he said, taking her in his arms and kissing her soundly.

He assured her that Fergus was well, although they were all exhausted and in need of rest and nourishment. "I saw Abe and decided I needed to come back home with him, but Fergus and the Paterson boys are riding out again soon with McDowell."

The men had brought a new gun along with the powder and ammunition. "Presents from your daughters," he told her. He related that McDowell's men had indeed stolen the horses at Allen's Mountain, but then the entire militia had to hightail it over the mountains to escape, up into the Watauga settlements.

He expressed his surprise and admiration for the ditch and abatis the women and single man had managed to construct, "but I fear they shall not be enough. While we were in the Overmountain settlements, we learned about a message Ferguson sent with a released prisoner, a cousin of Isaac Shelby's. It said that unless everyone over there surrenders, swears loyalty to the king, and moves back over to this side of the Blue Ridge, he's going to march his army over the mountains, burn their homes, hang their leaders, and in general lay waste the countryside 'with fire and sword,' I believe were his very words."

"Whooee," Billy exclaimed. "What're we gonna do?"

Will grinned. "I don't think Ferguson reckoned on the Overmountain people," he said. "They'll not tolerate his threats, and there are plans afoot to march against him. I came back to let you know what's going on, and to see if it would be wise for our family to go to the safety of the mountains until this is over."

Fiona snorted. "That doesn't sound so safe to me, not if that major makes good on his threats." She told him about Ferguson's visit, and that Carson and the Davidson brothers had supposedly taken the oath of allegiance to the king and were riding with Ferguson to steal cattle and swine, "and who knows what else?" she added, although that was all they'd asked of her. She wondered, however, if there were any peaches still in the orchard.

Will took her hand and gave it a hard squeeze. "I don't know what got into Carson and those Davidson boys. But I think they'll be sorry for that choice."

Fiona rubbed his fingers with her thumbs. "Do you really think anybody has a chance against the English? I mean, I've heard they're the most powerful army in the world."

Will leaned back against the rough wood chair and let out a sigh. "I don't know. But Shelby and old Daniel Morgan gave him a pounding over at Musgrove Mill. What I do know is that Ferguson thinks we're just operating as small bands of local militia and can't organize into a fighting force. But I can tell you firsthand, those old Indian fighters, John Sevier and the Shelbys and others, aren't about to roll over and give up."

Then he told her what else he knew of their plan to fight back.

"They're not ones to sit and wait for an attack," he said. "They're organizing to go after the redcoats. Shelby sent word to the leaders of five or six militias from as far away as Virginia to join the attack. They're planning to muster at Sycamore Shoals later this month." He paused, then added, "They're planning to fight or die," he told her. "And I plan to be with them, if this danged toe will let me march."

CHAPTER TWENTY-SEVEN

Sycamore Shoals, North Carolina, September 20, 1780

The insolent and provocative note sent from Ferguson by way of Isaac Shelby's cousin had just the opposite of its intended effect on the Overmountain people. Instead of frightening the settlers and cowing them into submission, Cass saw that it only served to rile them up and strengthen their resolve to go after the hated major and his army.

Cass and his sisters had been at John Sevier's home the day Shelby's cousin arrived with the vicious threatening message. Sevier's wife had died the year before, and in August he was remarrying, taking as his bride the young woman he'd saved at the battle of Caswell's Fort a few years back, the one called Bonny Cate Sherrill. The messenger had come riding hell bent for leather into the midst of the celebration, summoning his friend Sevier away from his own wedding party.

As part of Sevier's militia who were always on call to fight the constant Chickamauga threat, Cass soon learned the contents of that message, and what Shelby and Sevier planned to do about it. Now, he and hundreds of the rugged backwoodsmen were gathering at Sycamore Shoals, ready and anxious to fight Ferguson. They were going after him, taking their fight far away from their homes and farms, somewhere over the mountains. They were determined to find him. And kill him.

One of the concerns shared by everyone who lived in the Overmountain settlements was that the Chickamaugas would get wind of the upcoming march against Ferguson and attack them while their best fighters were away. Cass had spoken with his sisters about the risk they were taking in staying here and suggested they head further into Virginia, but they both adamantly declined.

"I can shoot as good as any man," Jeannette told him. "You know that."

Cass did know that. Jeannette had proven to be one of the best shooters in Watauga when she won a contest, competing against him and others whose skills with a firearm were respected.

Jeannette fascinated Cass. She'd changed so much from the sassy, impetuous girl who'd once made overtures toward him. He saw her now as a strong, handsome, and very brave woman, despite her penchant for wearing men's attire. She brooked no reproach from anyone, man or woman, white or red, and she was fiercely protective of Maura and little T.J.

Although her intention in coming into the mountains was to help make black powder, she'd found the work nauseating. The droppings of centuries of wild animals and bats from nearby caves had to be mined for the saltpeter needed for the process. The odor of the burning droppings overcame her from the first day, and she quickly changed to another endeavor needed for protection, one she had proven good at... gunsmithing.

Maura, however, seemed unfazed by the smell and the hot, dangerous work. T.J. played alongside the Patton daughters while Maura worked feverishly with Mary Patton to make as much powder as they could for the upcoming fight. She'd told Cass that Mary had promised John Sevier five hundred pounds of it by the twenty-fifth of the month, mustering day.

Cass wondered what their chances were against Ferguson. The British had won many battles in the south, including that devastating blow at Camden last month, but the Americans had managed a few victories of their own in recent weeks. Cass wished he could have been at Musgrove Mill to see the victory Isaac Shelby and old Colonel Daniel Morgan had pulled off there.

After the defeat of the British in that battle, apparently many of the partisans with Tory leanings had lost enthusiasm for their cause, which was another blow to Ferguson's plans and pride. But it had also ignited Ferguson's anger. Cass had no illusions that the haughty, prideful British major would do everything in his power to wreak revenge, including making good on his threatened invasion of the Overmountain settlements.

* * *

September 25, 1780

Cass rode among the men and their families gathered on the level grounds near Robertson's Fort at Sycamore Shoals. It was a cool September day with a light breeze fluttering the yellowing sycamore leaves high overhead. Wives and children had ridden with their menfolk to say their farewells, and despite the gravity of the occasion, most maintained a bright attitude. They visited among each other and shared food and camaraderie as if it were a Sunday afternoon picnic.

Cass looked over the gathering, his eyes searching for Fergus, who'd followed McDowell back to the Catawba Valley to try to recruit more men before turning around and coming back for the muster. Cass sighted the McDowell militia at a far end of the field and spurred his horse their way. He saw Fergus waving him over.

"Hey, Fergus," Cass said, reining in. "Glad to see you back. Is Will with you?"

"No. He stayed at the farm, trying to heal up that bad toe. He plans to catch up with us over in Quaker Meadows."

Cass gave a low laugh. "Seems kind of funny, McDowell from Quaker Meadows, has dragged all of you up the mountain only to go back down there again."

"He said he wanted to make sure the other colonels knew he was committed to this. Seems to be something of a rivalry among the main officers as to who's going to command this fight. He didn't want to let Shelby and Sevier one-up him. But he's already headed back down the mountain. He sent a message to Colonel Cleveland and Major Winston from over in Wilkes and Surry counties to meet up with us at Quaker Meadows, so he's gone back to make things ready." Fergus paused, then added, "Don't know why he's worried these others don't think he'd be in on this. There's not one of 'em more loyal to our cause than McDowell," he said. "I've seen him take on Tories and Brits alike all over our territory. He's a brave man. I'd follow him anywhere."

As they rode together, the Gordon brothers surveyed the gathering troops. "Over there's Colonel Campbell's men from up in Virginia," Cass said, pointing across the field. "He's brought four hundred men from over the Holston." He turned to Fergus. "How many you got with McDowell?"

"McDowell and Colonel Hampton from Tryon County together have about a hundred and sixty."

"Shelby and Sevier have almost five hundred between them. When Cleveland and Winston join us, there'll surely be hundreds more."

"McDowell guesses upward of three hundred fifty," Fergus told him, "And he expects others, like Pa, will join us as we go along."

Cass summed the numbers and came away impressed. What he didn't know, maybe nobody did, was how many Ferguson had on his force. They heard a commotion and turned to see what was happening, and a cheer went up when Mary Patton rode into their midst with a wagon load of the promised black powder. "Look! There's Maura!" Cass said, prodding his horse and heading toward them. "Come on!"

Maura followed the wagon on horseback. She was dirty, with a smudged face and hair tied back with a large kerchief. But she was smiling. "We did it!" she called out when she saw her brothers. "We got the five hundred pounds! Just finished it up last night in time to load."

The two men stared at their sister. Neither had ever seen her so disheveled. Or so jubilant.

"Amazing," Cass murmured. "Congratulations. Maura, you've likely helped save a lot of lives with this."

At that, tears rose in Maura's eyes. "I wish it could be otherwise, Cass. It seems we've done nothing all our lives but fight. I'm ready for a little peace."

"Amen," came a man's voice from just behind them. It was a man of the cloth, Cass saw by his attire, and he thought fleetingly about Jeannette. Since her terrible experience as the wife of a preacher, she seemed to hate them all. But this was the Reverend Doak, a young, well-educated parson who, unlike so many others in his profession, fervently espoused the cause of freedom. Cass had heard him speak at one of the settlement meeting houses and found his words compelling.

"Greetings, Reverend Doak," Cass said, then moved aside to let the black-clad clergyman pass.

"I share the woman's yearning for peace," Doak said, "but sometimes we must fight to achieve it. Blessings on you and all who are gathered here," he added, moving toward the river.

Cass watched him and again thought of Jeannette. He dismounted and went over to Maura and helped her out of the saddle. "Have you seen Jeannette?" he asked.

"Not since yesterday, but I'm sure she's around here somewhere."

Over a thousand fighters and their families were moving as a group toward the place where Reverend Doak would soon speak, and it was almost impossible to search out a single face. "Keep an eye out for her. I'd like to say goodbye."

The Reverend was a mighty speaker, and his voice reverberated over the crowd as he shared his conviction that the Lord was with this army, that their cause was righteous, and that their experience with fighting the Indians would serve them well in this battle. He spoke for nearly an hour, and looking around, Cass could see that the colonels were mounting now, anxious to get on the trail. It was almost noon, and it was going to be a long, slow ride with over a thousand men, wagons, and a large herd of beeves making their way down a narrow mountain trail.

At last, Doak cried out, "Hear the words of Gideon! When I blow with a trumpet, I and all that are with me, then blow ye the trumpets also on every side of all the camp and say, 'The sword of the Lord and of Gideon!'" He called out these last words three times, and the battle cry was taken up by the men who were now fired up and ready to fight.

CHAPTER TWENTY-EIGHT

On the hunt for Ferguson, September 26, 1780

The army that left Sycamore Shoals that day wasn't really an army. It was a force of rag-tag volunteers clad in fringed hunting shirts, leather pants, and moccasins or handmade boots, led by commanders of separate partisan militias. Some were seasoned Indian fighters, others, mostly the newcomers, hardly knew how to shoot. All of them, however, provided their own weapons—long rifles or muskets, with knives and tomahawks tucked into their belts. Their gear consisted for the most part of a blanket, drinking cup, and what food they could carry. Some were on horseback. Others walked along behind, keeping up as best they could.

They rested that evening at a large overhanging rock near Roan Mountain. When it began to rain, Sevier put the wagon carrying Mary Patton's precious powder, along with meal and other supplies, beneath the rock to keep it dry. The men slept that night under soggy blankets in the rain.

The cattle were proving to be a problem. They had brought hundreds of heads of cattle, and herding them along the narrow trail meant moving at a snail's pace. Part of the success of the plan depended on surprising Ferguson. Sevier was concerned that if they were too slow in arriving, he would learn of their plan and either attack them before they were ready, or worse, escape. Cass, being one of Sevier's preferred scouts, rode alongside him and heard him grumble.

"If we don't move faster than this, Ferguson will be an old man or already dead when we find him."

The officers met and made the decision to butcher some of the cattle, cook what meat they would probably need in the near future and send the rest of the herd back to the settlements.

"It won't be sufficient for the whole journey," Sevier said to Shelby, who was not convinced this was the right thing to do, "but we will surely find provisions along the way."

"Not in the manner of Ferguson, I hope," was Shelby's terse reply before riding off.

When they reached the bald of Roan Mountain the following afternoon, the rain turned to snow. Despite the ankle-deep drifts, the militia men were called to drill, something they were unaccustomed to, and roll was called. Two of Sevier's men did not answer, and Cass knew they were of Tory leaning. He heard a loud expletive from his commander.

"Those two are likely hightailing it down to find Ferguson and let him know we're coming," he growled. "We must move now as quickly as possible." Cass knew if Sevier caught them, they would be hanged on the spot.

Because of this defection, the commanding officers decided to change their route and split up as they headed over the edge of the escarpment. Colonel Campbell's Virginians descended through Turkey Cove; Shelby, Sevier, and those among McDowell's contingent went via the North Cove. Cass was able to ride with Fergus for much of this way, and they were camped together when Colonel McDowell rode into their midst. Cass marveled at the older man's ability to withstand what seemed to him like days in the saddle without a break.

"Good news!" he said cheerfully, as if he was greeting the men at a picnic. "Cleveland and Winston are already past Fort Defiance, well on their way to join us!" He accepted a cup of spring water, then added, "and, it looks like some men serving under Sumter down south have learned about our mission, and they too, might join us."

At this a cheer went up. The stronger their force, the better their chances, Cass thought.

* * *

Catawba Valley, September 29, 1780

As had happened before, Kate sensed her brothers' approach and gave the others notice.

Fiona hadn't felt their impending arrival, and she wondered at times if she'd lost some of her power of the Sight. She'd figured—hoped—that both Cass and Fergus would soon be headed this way, not from her Sight but rather from a recent visit from Colonel Joseph McDowell, Charles's younger brother. He was riding to let the neighboring farmers know that the large force of Overmountain men was coming their way, headed to Quaker Meadows, and to encourage any available men to join them.

She was dismayed but not surprised when Will assured McDowell that he would be on his way to meet up with them the next day. His toe was better now, but if he walked on it much, it flared up again. She'd heard him curse it out loud from time to time, but she knew he was not about to let it keep him from joining the fighting men on their way to rout the hated Major Ferguson.

"Ma! Pa! Katie!" Cass called out, followed by a loud 'Halloo!" from Fergus. They hitched their horses to a tree and ran up to the porch. The rain that had started at the outset of the march had followed them all the way, and they were soaked.

Fiona hugged them both, disregarding their wet clothes. "Come inside, quickly, before you catch your death…" She broke off there, thinking it an ill omen to say that, considering their mission. She handed each a dry cloth and hurried them to stand by the fire.

Will shook each of his son's hands so hard Fiona thought he might rip them from their arms. Kate, holding little Ben, danced around them like a sprite, and Alicia and Cissy brought some hot cider and fresh biscuits. Abe and Billy came at a run from the barn, picking up some more logs for the fire before they came into the warm cabin.

Once warmed and settled, Cass told them what was underway. "It's hard to believe," he said, "but Shelby and Sevier have managed to garner almost a thousand men, and they're on their way to meet up with another three hundred or so led by Ben Cleveland at Quaker Meadows. The colonels are all set on finding Ferguson and attacking him before he knows what's hit him."

Fergus spoke up. "Problem is trying to find him. McDowell sent a scout who came back reporting he was camped out at Gilbert Town."

"That could be," Fiona said, and told her sons about Hunting John's visit to their farm to move their livestock to safety. "He told me he thought they were at Gilbert Town."

She also told them about Ferguson's visit, and Carson's and the Davidsons's desertion.

But Cass only laughed. "You don't for one minute believe those boys turned Tory, do you, Ma?"

"It was hard for me, but there they were, right alongside that wretched Englishman."

Cass's eyes twinkled. "You're going to love this, Ma. Hunting John and others from up toward the Catawba headwaters made a plot to fool the Tories. Carson and the Davidson brothers agreed to sign the oath of allegiance to the king, which gave their family and properties protection from being raided and burned."

"Disgusting!" Fiona said, shaking her head. "What's there about this I'm going to love?"

"Well, it gave Hunting John and his boys time to take most of the livestock out of the valley and hide them away back in the coves. And when those three supposed turncoats went riding about with Ferguson, like when they came here, they were able to steer Ferguson away from the token cattle and hogs that had been left and toward a larger herd that could be easily had in the valley."

Fiona frowned, remembering John Carson saying something to that effect. "And...?"

"He sure enough took them to that herd, and his men were about done slaughtering near half of them when Carson sort of 'remembered' who they belonged to—Joseph Brown, Dement, and Johnstone!"

At this, Will broke out into hilarious laughter. "Tories! He led Ferguson to kill Tory beeves! I knew John Carson would never betray us."

"What happened to Carson?" Fiona asked, wondering if Ferguson would take retribution, but Cass didn't know.

"We just heard about this before we left, so we don't know what happened to Carson and them Davidson boys. But Ferguson got his provisions, one way or the other."

Cass and Fergus stayed only long enough to dry off and eat a hearty meal, feed their horses, and kiss the family goodbye. Fiona watched with deep sorrow as they rode away in search of the enemy and its hated leader. Would she see them alive again? She turned to find Will taking down his gun and gathering his belongings.

"So, you are really going, with that bad toe and all?"

"You know I am. And don't try to stop me. If my children can step up to this fight, I'm not about to sit here and let them go it alone."

Without a word, Fiona gave Alicia and Cissy a nod. "Get his provisions together. And enough for the rest of us to get to Quaker Meadows with him." She turned to Will and touched his shoulder. "I understand, Will Gordon." Then in Gaelic, she said, "You must promise to return to me whole and sound."

He gave a low laugh and replied in Gaelic, "May the gods let it be."

* * *

Fiona, Kate, Alicia, and Cissy carrying her little boy rode over to Quaker Meadows in the wagon, with Will, Abe, and Billy on horseback. In the wagon was the new gun that Will had brought from Jeannette, and as much ammunition as they felt they could spare and still leave enough for Fiona to protect their farm if need be. They arrived just as the long contingent of soldiers came down the mountain to be welcomed by the McDowell brothers, with beef from cattle brought out of the mountain coves roasting over bonfires built from their own fencing.

Others, like Will, trickled in, some not aligned with any particular militia, but determined to join this march to free themselves not only of the English, but maybe even more so of their Tory tormentors. Will spied John Carson and four of the Davidsons, including the two who had supposedly been turncoats, riding up, and he hailed them. "I knew you weren't with them," he said to the men as they approached.

"We could stand accused of that, I suppose," John Carson replied with a sigh. "It wasn't something we wanted to do, but it was part of the plan, and it appears to have worked," he added, brightening and sweeping his arm toward the meat cooking over the fire. "Otherwise, they'd have had this feast instead of us." Fiona hadn't liked the plan, but she had to agree with Carson, it appeared to have worked.

As did some of the other plans laid by the officers leading the attack. That night, those from Wilkes and Surry counties arrived, swelling the numbers camped out on the flat meadow to nearly fifteen hundred.

Fiona and the women left the men and took the wagon to Mrs. McDowell's house where they were warmly welcomed by the colonel's mother, the first McDowell wife to dare settle in this hostile land. "Those damned Tories, they came and tore up my house and plundered my stores, and they set about making threats about my sons," the widowed Mrs. McDowell raved.

"Said they'd kill Charles outright, and make Joseph plead on his knees for his life, but then they'd kill him anyway." She was overwrought, and Fiona went to her.

"We're hoping this journey will bring this all to an end," she said, trying to soothe the old woman, who suddenly fell into Fiona's arms, sobbing.

"I pray you are right. My husband is dead, and both my sons are in the face of danger every day. I don't know how much longer I can take this."

With Fiona's entire family now engaged in this war, be it against the British major or the Indians, she couldn't agree more. She said nothing, but just held the woman for a long while, taking her own consolation from the human warmth of their embrace.

CHAPTER TWENTY-NINE

On the road to Kings Mountain, September 30, 1780

W ill rejoined his militia group under Charles McDowell, riding alongside Fergus as they left Quaker Meadows. Cass had been summoned by Sevier and rode with that contingent. It had been difficult to bid farewell to Fiona, but she had smiled bravely despite the tears that obviously threatened. It must be so hard on her, he reflected as he rode, with the three men in her family on this march, and her daughters up in the highlands, possibly facing Indian attack.

Years had passed since Will began his quest for freedom, and still it remained just out of reach. Freedom's edge. He recalled Rutherford's words. Would this gathering of determined settlers marching toward highly trained British troops be able to pull off their attack and bring freedom closer to their reach? The colonels all seemed to agree that killing Patrick Ferguson would take some of the wind out of Cornwallis's sails. If they were successful, the next target, Will thought, should be Tarleton, the butcher. And then Rawdon.

He reined in his angry thoughts. First things first. They must get Ferguson.

* * *

October 1-2, 1780

They camped that night at Bedford Hill, and the rains came again. Taking what shelter they could beneath trees, the men huddled in the cold and damp. At daylight, they rose, expecting to march on, but to Will's surprise and dismay, the officers seemed hesitant to go forward without a clear leader in charge. There were now five colonels, each in command of separate militias. There was no true unified army on this march. Up until now, the colonels had taken turns, changing commands daily. But they agreed that they needed a single leader to guide the endeavor forward.

"Let us send to General Gates for an official commanding officer," one of the colonels suggested, but Shelby would have none of it.

"What? And lose any advantage of surprise we might have? No. We have experienced leaders here, and we must move on."

In the end, they agreed to send one of the colonels, Charles McDowell, to Hillsborough with this request. Then they elected William Campbell as commanding officer in the meantime.

Campbell was not only imminently qualified from his previous military service, but he'd also brought the largest force on this march.

Later, Cass who had witnessed this meeting, told Will and Fergus that another reason was Campbell was the only one not from North Carolina, so putting the command in his hands should avoid jealousy among the others. In Charles McDowell's absence, his younger brother, Major Joseph McDowell, would command that militia.

After camping two days in the rain, the men were nervous and irritable. Some made overtures that they were going back to their families. Before moving on toward Gilbert Town, where they believed their quarry to be, the colonels and other officers assembled their troops for a meeting, and Will watched, fascinated, as the very rotund Colonel Ben Cleveland gave a soundly patriotic call for the men to rally not just for the freedom this could bring, but also for the protection of their families. The older man must have weighed two hundred and fifty pounds, but he seemed to have the energy of a fit younger man.

Cleveland then offered the weak-hearted a chance to back out. No one moved, but Joseph McDowell spoke up too, asking, "what would the home folks say if you arrived there safely while others bravely fought for their country?" Again, no one moved, and silence prevailed. Then Shelby stepped forward. "Our force must be solid," he said. "Any man who desires to leave, take three steps backward now."

Not a man moved, and slowly applause built among the troops, filling them, Will believed, with the first sign of true unity among the disparate militia units.

* * *

October 4, 1780

Afterward, they moved on, only to find upon arriving at Gilbert Town that their bird had flown, headed, it was rumored, for the British fort at Ninety-Six in South Carolina.

During their overnight at Gilbert Town, Major William Candler and a force of thirty Georgians marched into camp, bringing with them the story of George Clarke's defeat and retreat at Augusta. "What's left of them is headed over the mountains," Candler told the officers. "Mostly women, children, old people, some of them barely alive."

This tale spread through the camp, embellished by details of the capture, torture or hanging of the patriots that fought with Clarke in Georgia, details that served to strengthen the determination of the Americans to take revenge on Ferguson.

* * *

October 5, 1780

Following what they perceived to be the path of Ferguson's retreat from Gilbert Town, the growing army made its way to Alexander's Ford and camped on a farm near the Green River.

By this time, Will's toe was swollen and inflamed, making it nearly impossible for him to walk. He wondered what help he would be in the upcoming battle. Or if instead he would he be a hindrance.

He had tried to hide his pain by remaining mounted for as long as he could, but when he got off his horse at this latest encampment, he stumbled and nearly fell. Excruciating pain shot through him as he righted himself using his horse, but Fergus had seen him and ran to his Pa.

"Ma told me you shouldn't have come," his son said, taking Will's arm and draping it over his shoulder, helping him to take a seat on a log.

Will sat in silence, cursing the day he'd dropped that stone, the *clach cuid fìr*, on his foot when he was sixteen. Cursing his stubbornness in insisting on coming along on this march, knowing this might happen.

Cursing himself for not listening to Fiona when she told him he was needed just as much at home, protecting her and their farm.

Just cursing. To himself. And wondering what the hell he should do now?

As if in answer, the colonels gathered in a staff meeting, and Cass reported later that they decided that the very size of the force and the stress of the long journey, especially on those who had come on foot, was slowing them down too much. Ferguson had several days lead on them, and they wanted to speed up the chase. "They're choosing the best riflemen and strongest horses to continue," he told his stepfather and Fergus. "They want the foot soldiers and those with horses that are too tired to follow more slowly and serve as a rear guard."

That night, as the officers made the rounds of the various militias and tried to ascertain who were the best to take on ahead, Will heard a commotion on the heavily guarded perimeter of the camp. A Colonel Lacey of Sumter's men, he learned, had ridden in, and been mistaken for a Tory spy, until he related having met up with Charles McDowell on his way to Hillsborough and learned about this march. He brought news of Ferguson's location, and further, promised to lead his force of South Carolinians to join them the following day at Cowpens, about twenty miles further on.

* * *

Quaker Meadows, North Carolina, October 6, 1780

"I can bear it no longer," Fiona told Alicia in private. "We've waited here for a week with no word. I think Will believed this would all be over in a few days, but something's telling me it's not over yet." She paused and looked at the other woman. "That's not all. It's Will. He isn't going to make it, unless..."

"Unless you go to him?" Alicia said. She had been with Fiona since she was a young girl, and by now she seemed to know her thoughts as if she, too, had the Sight.

Fiona nodded. "I want to take the wagon and go after him," she stated, brooking no argument, although Alicia rarely did that. "Will you go with me?"

"Of course, I will. But what of Katie and Cissy and the men?" The entire family had remained at the McDowell plantation after the army had departed, helping Mrs. McDowell and the wives of her two sons return the place to rights, and consoling all the wives and families who had come to see the men off on their journey.

"I don't want them left alone at our farm, so I'll ask Mrs. McDowell if they can stay here until we return."

"How're we going to find Mister Will and the boys?" Alicia asked.

Fiona looked at her as if she'd lost her mind. "Following fifteen hundred soldiers, most on horseback, shouldn't be so hard. Horses have a way of leaving their sign." At that, both women laughed and made ready to head out in search of Will. As always, Fiona carried the now nearly worn-out woolen satchel that had come with her from Ireland, medicinal herbs and tinctures, bandages, and scissors within its scruffy hold.

CHAPTER THIRTY

Cowpens, South Carolina, October 6, 1780

Cowpens was so named because the owner, an English Tory, had a large cattle ranch there and had built numerous pens to herd his animals. When they arrived, the Tory was interrogated, but he claimed he didn't know Ferguson's whereabouts, said the British hadn't passed by his place. Shelby and Sevier were doubtful the man was telling the truth, but in any case, they gave orders to commandeer many of the beeves to feed the tired, hungry soldiers now camped on the grounds.

Cass remained with Will until he saw that he was settled and made as comfortable as possible, considering the cold and persistent rain that seemed to aggravate his already painful toe. Will had protested that he could go on, but Major McDowell forbade it, and Will did not put up much argument.

Colonel Lacey and the rest of the South Carolinians arrived as promised, as did an unexpected visitor, a lame spy who had recently passed himself off as a Tory and mingled with enemy soldiers long enough to learn where Ferguson was now located. "He's camped up there on Kings Mountain," he reported. "Taking the high ground. Thinks he can hold off any attack from there."

Kings Mountain, although not far away, was in the opposite direction of Ninety-Six.

They had almost gone the wrong way. They must turn east and make haste. The officers quickly determined to move out that very night. Over nine hundred horsemen and the best marksmen in the joint militias left Cowpens after dark, marching through rain and slush toward Kings Mountain. Cass bade Will goodbye and moved on with Sevier's men.

"We'll have that Brit before you know it," he'd assured Will as he took his leave. "I'll see you when the smoke clears." Then he nodded toward a piece of the beef that Will had set aside for later. "Save me a bite of that, will you? I'll come for it when I can."

Fergus and the younger Paterson men, Jake, Joe, and David, were riding with McDowell's militia, but Cass was glad that George had volunteered to remain with Will. "I'm not old yet," he'd said, "but I'm getting there. I'll tend to Will here, and any others who need helpin' out. We'll be along behind you, just a little slower."

The march was wet and exhausting, and at one point, Sevier, Campbell, and Cleveland proposed a stop to give men and horses a much-needed rest. Shelby all but exploded at the thought. "I will not stop until night, even if I follow Ferguson into Cornwallis's lines!"

The march continued.

Two Tories were captured along the way, both of whom confirmed that Ferguson was indeed atop Kings Mountain, and with a little intimidating encouragement from Colonel Campbell, agreed to guide them there. At another house along the way, one of their own spies was discovered having dinner with some Tory ladies. Knowing the spy was loyal, probably just hungry, Sevier allowed some of his younger officers to have a little fun in "rescuing" him. Upon their return, spy in hand, Cass heard their story.

"We made a big show of finding him and accusing him of being a Tory spy," one of them said. "He knew we was funnin' him, and played along, screaming his head off and begging us not to hang him. We brought in a rope and threatened to do just that, putting a noose around his neck. I thought those ladies were going to swoon!" he added with a laugh. The men had carried on how they'd take him away and hang him out of sight of the women. Then they'd all had a good laugh as soon as they were away from the house.

The spy in question was Enoch Gilmer, as loyal a patriot as ever there was, who had given valuable service to the officers in charge. And he'd learned more over his interrupted home cooked dinner. "Them ladies took some chickens up to Ferguson just this morning," he said. "Told me exactly how to get up there between two creeks where there's a hunting camp."

"I know the place," Major Chronicle said. "Been there myself several times."

Before moving on, the officers withdrew to discuss their plan of action. Major Chronicle, who was from this area and knew the low ridge called Kings Mountain, suggested they surround the rise at its base, making escape impossible. Campbell agreed, reminding them of Reverand Doak's speech: *"then blow ye the trumpets also on every side of all the camp and say, 'The sword of the Lord and of Gideon!'"*

The officers quickly honed this plan—they would place the individual militias at strategic positions on every side of the foot of the mountain where Ferguson was camped, and attack in turns to give one a chance to retreat and reload to attack again. Most importantly, no one was to attack before all were in place and the signal was given.

Sevier gathered his men, most of them hardened Indian fighters, and drew a sketch of the plan in the mud. "They're up here, on the top of this hill," he said, drawing an outline of the layout as he understood it from Chronicle's description. "We're to go here," he told them, pointing to the assigned location. "We'll be between Shelby and Campbell. The Holston men will go first. When you hear their Indian war whoops, you'll know it's the signal for you to advance up the hill, taking cover behind the trees, and retreating as necessary."

"So we'll be shooting uphill?" one of the men asked.

"That's right. Less chance of us shooting one another. And with the Brits shooting downhill, they're likely to overshoot. We'll do it like we always have, boys, Indian style. And," he added grinning, "make sure you yell like Indians. I heard it scares the dickens out of Tories."

The sun finally came out about noon, and Cass felt his spirits lift. Good omens seemed everywhere, and they continued to appear. They captured two more Tories that morning, as well as a young man named Ponder who was carrying a message to Cornwallis, a fervent plea for help from Ferguson. "Well, this is good news," Sevier said, grinning broadly. "Tell me, sir," he asked the terrified messenger, "what does our good friend Ferguson look like?"

The man considered this a moment, then said, "He's impeccable."

"What?"

"I mean, he's always impeccably dressed. In fact, when he goes into battle, he covers his nice uniform with a red checkered duster."

Cass's eyes widened. "So, we shoot for the checkerboard," he blurted, almost laughing. "Makes an easy target." The captured man blanched, immediately seeing his mistake.

The groups separated and silently went about reaching their posts. All but the leaders tied their horses at the base of the mountain and secured their coats and blankets to the saddles. All they had with them were their guns, shot pouches, black powder, knives, and tomahawks. Excitement raced through Cass as the reality of battle came upon him.

Reaching their assigned area, he secured a position behind a large tree and looked to his right to see if he could locate Fergus, the Patersons, or the Davidson boys, but the McDowell militia were somewhere further around the mountain. To his immediate right, he saw Campbell's Virginia troops, and one in particular caught his eye. It was a slender young man with a big slouch hat, but it was his rifle that captured his attention. He could swear it was one of Jeannette's manufacture, like the one Will had brought with him. He smiled. Jeannette hated that she couldn't come along on this fight because she was a woman. He'd have to tell her that with her gunsmithing, she'd made it to the battle after all.

CHAPTER THIRTY-ONE

Kings Mountain, South Carolina, October 7, 1780

Cass heard a shot ring out. One of Ferguson's pickets must have spied them, so the major had warning, and they'd lost their advantage of surprise. Or almost, he thought, considering they were mostly in place by now. Those who had the farthest to go might not yet be to their stations, but the battle was on. The sound of drums came next as Ferguson alerted his troops, followed by several shrills blasts from a whistle, the noise shattering the air.

After that, all hell broke loose.

The troops had been admonished to wait until they heard Campbell's signal, and it came loud and clear: "Shout like hell and fight like devils!"

And they did.

With fierce bloodcurdling screams, a terrifying practice learned from years of fighting the Indians, Campbell's men made their way up the hill, taking shots and picking off the redcoats at the top with experienced accuracy until they needed to reload. The British, ever fond of their bayonets, surged down the hill after the retreating patriots. But as they reached the bottom, they heard another shrill whistle, turned, and ran back up to the top. They were easy pickings for those Holston boys who had already reloaded.

Cass heard similar yells from the other side of the mountain where Shelby's men were poised, and he was itching to join the fray. Only Colonel Sevier's discipline as a fighter kept his men at bay until he was ready. Instead, he ordered them to steadily inch their way up the hill, between Campbell's and Shelby's forces, while the redcoats were occupied by them. As he made his way from tree to tree, Cass could hear the other units attacking from the far side of the small mountain. The smoke was so thick, Cass could barely see, but as they neared the crest, he made out the figures of several riders, one of them clad in a red checkered overcoat.

Ferguson!

Cass could scarcely believe his eyes. The famed and hated major was trying to make a break for it, racing down the hill through enemy lines, leaving his fighters to themselves at the summit. Three other officers, easily identifiable as such from their uniforms, rode with him. Cass saw the major raise his sword and shout something before he was hit with a hail of bullets. He fell from his horse, his foot entangled in the stirrup, and was dragged downhill by the frightened animal. Two of the others had been hit as well, falling cleanly to the ground. Cass took a bead on the third, a large-bodied man with gray hair. His shot hit the mark, direct to the heart, and the officer fell.

The battle was over in little more than an hour, and as the smoke cleared, Cass heard the anguished cries of the wounded as he stepped over the bodies of the dead. Smoke from the gunfire seared his throat and burned his eyes. Many of the mountain fighters were running downhill to where Ferguson's body had been taken, wanting to make sure that their target, the main reason they had come here, was indeed dead.

Instead, Cass made his way steadily toward the body of the officer he had shot. He had killed his share of Indians when riding with Sevier in the Cherokee wars, and he believed today he had taken out a number of the British and Tories who fought with Ferguson. Why then, was he so drawn to look upon this one? Was it just because of his status as an officer?

The man was heavy set and had a pudgy face, now drained of all color. His hat lay on the ground nearby, as did his weapon. Cass collected both before kneeling beside the man. He looked rather old to be fighting a battle like this, he considered, but then, Ben Cleveland and Colonel Hambright were of this age as well. He noted the dead officer's hands, how small they were. Reaching for his lapel, he pulled back the blood-soaked red coat and saw that his bullet had entered the heart dead on. Blood blossomed on his white waistcoat.

They had been told that should they emerge victorious they could claim weapons and other spoils of war. There, lying against this man's waistcoat, gleaming in the sun, was a large, gold watch.

"Go ahead," a voice came to him from behind. "Take it. You shot him. It's yours." He turned to see Colonel Campbell riding up the mountain toward where the British prisoners were being assembled. A few shots continued to ring out. "I must put a stop to the fighting now," he said. "Collect what you can of value off him." With that, he rode on.

Feeling somewhat like a thief, Cass nonetheless began to search the man's pockets but found nothing of much value. He took the watch, his musket and bayonet, and his hat. Turning, he almost ran smack into the boy with the slouch hat he'd seen earlier brandishing a gun he thought might have been crafted by Jeannette. He was with two others, following Campbell up the hill.

"Sorry," he said, looking into the boy's face that was smeared with mud and smoke.

Suddenly, he recognized the face, and he jumped back as if he'd been burned. "Jeannette!"

Jeannette Gordon took off the large floppy hat and grinned at her stepbrother. "Guess I don't need to keep up this disguise any longer."

"What in tarnation...how...?"

Jeannette was clad in leather pants, knee-high boots, and a fringed hunting shirt, like most of the rest of the Overmountain men. At her waist she had a knife and a tomahawk. With the hat covering her face, she easily passed as just another fighting man from the backcountry.

"I told you I wanted to join this fight. I met up with these two at the muster, told them what I wanted to do, and they agreed to help me." She introduced the other two soldiers. "This is David and William Ward, from up in Virginia. "It was because of them I was able to keep my secret. They stood guard when I...you know...had to go off into the woods..."

David Ward shook Cass's hand. "This is one hell of a fighting woman," he said, grinning. "Best shot I ever saw."

Cass remained speechless as William Ward took his hand as well. "I think she picked off at least eight of 'em on the hill there," he told Cass.

Jeannette said nothing, just stared at Cass, as if defying him to scold her for her deceit.

Finally, Cass found his tongue. "I guess you know Will and George stayed behind with the foot soldiers," he said, wondering if he was trying to make her feel guilty for leaving her father behind.

"I know," she said without emotion. "It was for the best. That toe of his is giving him grief. He should never have come on this."

Absentmindedly, Cass put the gold watch in his pocket. He handed the rifle to David Ward, and then placed the dead man's hat on Jeannette's dark hair. "I think you earned this," he said, and meant it. If he'd had respect for Jeannette Gordon before, it paled to what he felt about her now. Impulsively, he pulled her into his arms and held her tight.

"I just thank God you weren't hurt."

Jeannette returned his embrace. "And I you."

* * *

In just sixty-five minutes, this raggedy group of volunteer soldiers with no military training killed almost three hundred British soldiers and wounded another hundred and sixty-three.

They took almost seven hundred prisoners. Among their own forces, they lost only twenty-eight, with sixty wounded. Among the casualties was Robert Sevier, brother to Colonel John Sevier, and the two majors, Chronicle and Mattox, who with their local knowledge of the hunting camp on Kings Mountain, had successfully guided them toward Ferguson.

CHAPTER THIRTY-TWO

October 11, 1780

Fiona and Alicia had followed the horse patties all the way to Gilbert Town, their wagon becoming mired in the mud several times, slowing their progress. Rain had pelted them for the first part of their journey, and they'd stopped for the night at several friendly farms along the way. They had brought provisions given them by the always generous McDowells, but Fiona was unsure if they had sufficient to sustain them for many more days.

They were about to proceed along the well-defined path that the men had taken, when they saw a woman on horseback riding toward them at a gallop from the south. She was disheveled and appeared frightened, and Fiona trusted no one these days.

"Halt!" she cried, standing up in the wagon and raising her rifle.

The woman reined in. "Don't shoot. I mean no harm."

Fiona did not lower the gun, but demanded, "Identify yourself. Who are you?"

"Name's Paul. They call me Virginia Paul."

"Where have you come from?"

"Over at Kings Mountain." At this the woman began to cry. "It was a terrible fight, and lots were kilt," she said. "I barely escaped with my life."

Fiona's heart began to pound, and she exchanged glances with Alicia. "Who was fighting?"

"Ferguson. And those wild yelling boys from over the back country."

Fiona was almost afraid to ask the next question. "And who won?"

"The yelling boys. I hightailed it out of there when they kilt Ferguson, but I almost got caught taking this horse."

Fiona was overjoyed to hear this news, but she worked to maintain a fierce countenance.

"You stole that horse?"

The woman looked at her defiantly. "Better than being captured and raped, maybe even hung. I was Ferguson's laundry woman. What chance you think I'd have if they caught me?"

Her reference to rape stung Fiona in the nether depths of her soul. She knew that rape was a weapon of war, as surely as a bayonet.

"You're a Tory. Are you trying to reach your Tory friends around here? There's lots of them in these parts, you know."

"I'm not a Tory, and I want no part of this here war no more. I want to just ride away and disappear." She looked nervously over her shoulder. "They're not far behind me. Please, lady, don't shoot me. Let me go. I done nothin' wrong but wash that man's duds. For me, it was a job, and the pay was good."

Fiona understood that women sometimes took on work for folks they didn't necessarily like, just to get by. And she understood this woman's fear of being raped. She gestured with her head in the direction of the road they had just come down. "Get on, then. Just don't expect much of a welcome from the neighbors who aren't Tories. There's lots of them in these parts as well."

She watched until the woman's figure disappeared in the distance, then sat back down on the hard wagon bench, trying to think. "She said they weren't far behind her," she said to Alicia.

"Maybe we should just stop here and bide awhile," Alicia replied. "See if they come along."

Fiona closed her eyes and summoned forth an image of Will. Was he alive? And Fergus?

And Cass? In her inner vision, she felt more than saw the sway of a horse's back as if she were a rider. Felt the rhythm of the animal. Felt Will coming home to her. But fear filled her when no images of her sons came to her. "Let's go on ahead," she said, taking the reins. For she had another feeling as well. She would be needed. There were many wounded coming with him.

It wasn't long until they crossed over a low hill and saw below them a long line of men—hundreds it looked like—and horses, and a few wagons, headed toward them on the rutted road.

Some of the horses carried a tandem litter between them, bearing the injured. The road being filled with the returning soldiers and their prisoners, there was no way for her to get the wagon through to find her family, so she drew to one side and waited.

The soldiers turned off into a field at the bottom of the hill to make camp for the night. Fiona eased the wagon back onto the road, moving slowly toward them, eyes searching desperately for Will and her sons. She saw George Paterson first, on foot, and then Will on his horse riding just behind. Another rider was alongside Will, but he wore a floppy, wide-brimmed hat she didn't recognize. She didn't think it was Cass or Fergus.

When at last she was able to maneuver the wagon down the hill and across the field to where she thought she'd seen Will and George go, she saw many men limping, bandaged, and some even still bleeding. Those on the tandem litters were being made as comfortable as possible when laid upon the soggy earth. The sky was clear now, but in October, that generally meant a cold night to come.

"There they are!" Alicia cried suddenly, and Fiona looked in the direction she pointed.

Relief rushed through her to see Cass and Fergus were now with Will. Two of George's boys were there as well. Others from McDowell's militia milled around together, some of them attempting to build a fire. Fiona had brought some of the wooden fence rails from Quaker Meadows, thinking firewood might be needed, and she'd been right. She steered the wagon directly toward her menfolk, apologizing briefly to any who she had to ask to move out of her way.

"Will! Cass! Fergus!" she cried, handing the reins to Alicia and jumping down from the wagon and running to them.

All of them, including the stranger in the big hat, turned to stare at her in amazement.

Then Will opened his arms, and she flew into them, breathless with relief. "Thank God you are well," she said, pulling back only long enough to kiss his mouth. She saw how drawn and pale he looked. She traced the tired lines on his face. "You are well, aren't you?"

He gave her a barely perceptible nod. "I'm well. My toe isn't so good, though. They made me stay behind. I never saw the fight. Stupid toe!"

Before she could ask any more about it, her boys broke in with hugs and greetings of their own, and then they stood back, grinning, as if they had a joke on her. Walking slowly up from behind, the soldier in the big hat took it off and gave her a radiant smile.

Fiona was astounded. "Jeannette! What are you doing here?"

The young woman in men's clothing gave her stepmother a powerful embrace. "They say I'm the best shot 'round these mountains," she said. "I made some guns, Maura made some black powder, but the boys here were putting their lives up for this fight. Figured the least I could do was take my own gun, some of Maura's black powder, and join the march."

Fiona just shook her head, still trying to understand what this strong-willed girl...no...this strong-willed woman had become. She should have been angry with her, but instead, she found she was rather proud. But she was still thunderstruck by it all. She had searched her Sight to find her husband and her sons. It never occurred to her to look for Jeannette alongside them.

Once she recovered somewhat from her shock, she managed to say, "I heard Ferguson was killed, and that you 'yelling boys' won the day."

Fergus smiled, but there was something sad about it. "That we did, Ma. The plan was brilliant, and it worked, and that old devil lies in his grave on top of that mountain he thought couldn't be taken."

There was something he wasn't saying. "Who was hurt? Was anybody killed?"

George Paterson, with Jake and David, were standing behind the Gordon men. When she asked this, Fergus stepped back and asked George to talk to his mother.

"Joe was hit," he said brusquely. "We've carried him this far in yonder litter between us."

His eyes teared up, and Fiona saw they were red and raw. "Don't know if he'll make it."

"Bring him here, now!" Fiona ordered, "and everyone else help me unload the wagon."

They laid Joe Paterson on the flat bottom of the wagon. He was seriously injured from a bullet that had ripped through his shoulder. "It didn't hit his vital parts," Fiona said to George as she surveyed his wound. "That's encouraging. But looks like he's lost a lot of blood."

"Is...is he going to die?" George asked. The other Paterson men were leaning over the edge of the wagon, looking at their brother.

"Only God knows," Fiona uttered, washing the wound with cold water from a nearby creek and applying the yellow powder she knew worked to prevent infection. Afterwards, she bandaged the wound and made a makeshift sling from a piece of canvas that had covered the goods she'd brought in the wagon. "I'll bring him home in the wagon. All that jostling in the litter didn't do him any good."

After she had done all she could for Joe, who had passed out during her ministrations, she asked the others to help put together a meal from the provisions she'd brought. "We'll be over to the fire shortly," she said, indicating with her head for Jeannette and the others to leave her alone with Will. When they turned to their duties, Fiona took Will to the back of the wagon and made him sit on the tailgate while she inspected his toe. She tried to hold back a grimace when she saw the raw, red skin scraped almost to the bone. It oozed and looked infected, far worse than the bullet wound in Joe's shoulder.

Again, she fetched the yellow powder from her satchel and reached for the water jug to wash the toe. Will grimaced with pain but said nothing. At last, she bound the toe and wrapped his foot tightly in a bandage as well.

"I can't walk in this contraption," Will complained.

"If you don't stay off that foot, you'll likely not be able to walk at all, Will Gordon."

They stayed the night in the open field, Will and Fiona bedding down in the wagon beside the inert figure of Joe Paterson. Alicia and Jeannette took shelter beneath the wagon. Cass went to report to Colonel Sevier and offer help with the hundreds of prisoners, and they didn't see him until the next day. Fergus milled around with the McDowell militia for a while, but after dark, he joined his family, rolling up in his blanket in the cold, damp night.

The night virtually vibrated with the sounds of hundreds of tired, war-torn men struggling to get some rest, many of them unsure what the morrow would bring. Many feared that when Cornwallis learned of this defeat, he would soon be in hot pursuit.

In the morning, as they were preparing to take Will and Joe back home, Cass came riding over to the wagon. "Can I have a word, Ma?" He dismounted and led her away from the wagon and out of earshot of anyone else. "I've something to show you," he said. "Colonel Campbell said because I shot the man this belonged to, it was mine for the taking. But somehow, I feel like a thief."

With that, he withdrew from his pocket the large gold watch he'd taken from the dead British officer and handed it to Fiona. She looked down at it. It seemed to sear her skin, and she nearly dropped it. She knew this watch. She was suddenly wrenched back to Edgewater plantation, to Nigel Stainton's office, and his cruel rapes with that big, gold watch in front of her face. She startled to tremble. "You say you killed this man?" she managed.

"I'm sure it was my bullet put him on the ground," Cass said, sounding proud. "He was a big kind of fellow, with gray hair and strangely small hands."

Fiona's own hands shook as she turned the watch over. Engraved on the back were the initials "N.S."

She swallowed hard and handed the watch back to her son. "Don't feel guilty for keeping it," she said, looking him directly in the eye. "It's your legacy, hard won at that battle."

CHAPTER THIRTY-THREE

Catawba Valley, North Carolina, Christmas 1780

Fiona, Kate, Alicia, and Cissy fetched ivy and holly berries from the woods and adorned their cabins in as festive a manner as they could, although Fiona didn't feel very festive. After the glow of the victory at Kings Mountain subsided, reality had returned. The Patriots were still at war with the British, although Ferguson's loss was an enormous setback to their attempt to conquer the south. And they were still plagued by the Indians, who continued to attack the westernmost settlements in the most vicious manner, fully supplied with British arms, ammunition, and provisions.

After a short reprieve and a visit home, Cass and Jeannette headed back to the Watauga settlements. Fergus stayed closer to home but preferred to remain on duty with Colonel and Major McDowell, who were also their friends and neighbors. She hadn't heard anything from Maura, but Jeannette had promised to see to her well-being and that of little T.J. Fiona wondered what the future held for those two in this backcountry conflict.

Will's toe had not healed. It had, in fact, turned a vicious shade of brownish purple and black, and Fiona knew the infection could spread throughout his body. The only way to save his life was to amputate the toe. She also knew she wasn't the one to do the job. She was a healer, had become known in the region as a granny woman, but a surgeon she was not. The closest one they knew of was in Salisbury, but it was a dangerous ride between their farm and that community, with Tories still loyal to Cornwallis seething over their loss at Kings Mountain and roaming the piedmont seeking revenge.

It was Fergus who offered to go for help. "Pa's in no shape to make that trip," he told his parents. "Jake and David said they'd go with me to fetch a surgeon."

"Just make sure it's not that old drunkard," Will said from where he lay on their bed.

Fiona knew he meant it in jest, but she didn't find it funny. Nothing about that episode with Jeannette's preacher husband was funny. She wondered if they'd ever find out what happened to Philemon Means. Jeannette had told her she'd likely never marry again, at least not until she knew Means was dead and buried.

The young men returned within a week, riding hard, with Dr. Gregory, the surgeon, alongside them. Will had continued to grow weaker and was almost incoherent with fever and pain by the time they arrived. The surgeon gave Will a generous dose of his own liquid corn, asked the young men to hold him down, and with the chop of a large knife, removed the toe as Will passed out. He gave Fiona medicine that was supposed to kill the infection if it had spread.

After the operation, Fiona and Dr. Gregory went out to the porch to get some fresh air. "Will he live?" she asked.

"Time will tell. He's a strong man, has a good family. Lot to live for. Sometimes that makes a difference."

She broached another subject. "Have you lived in Salisbury long, Doctor?"

He told her he'd been there since the former doctor had taken off. "Damned old Tory. Good riddance, I say. You should hear the stories people told me of his medical treatments. Shameful."

"Did anyone ever find out what happened to him? I hear he left town with the Tory preacher," Fiona pressed.

"I knew them both briefly. They left Salisbury and took up in Lincoln County, where I lived at the time. That place was infested with Tories, which I detest, and when I learned that Salisbury was without a doctor, I moved there. I heard Means got shot at that skirmish at Ramsour's Mill, and that the old doctor was too drunk to treat those who were wounded. I'm pretty sure Means died of his wounds."

'Pretty sure' was good enough for Fiona. It was what she would tell Jeannette. It was time for that woman to get on with her life. Dr. Gregory had also told them that sadly, old Hiram Greenlee had succumbed to pneumonia the previous winter.

Now, as Christmas approached, Will was recovering, but to Fiona's mind, he was a shadow of the vibrant, healthy man she'd always known. The doctor had told her he might walk again, but always with a crutch or cane. Thank goodness for Billy and Abe. They were strong and enjoyed working on the farm, which was a good thing, since it appeared that Will would no longer be able to.

Fiona wanted to make this Christmas something special for Will. She'd had Abe and Billy slaughter one of the hogs that had been spared when John Carson urged Ferguson to leave them behind for better herds. Fat pumpkins had filled their garden in the fall. Yams, turnips, and apples had been stored in the root cellar, beans and leather britches had been dried, and corn meal was ground over at the Paterson place for bread.

She had invited the Patersons to come for Christmas dinner. They were now a large and lively bunch, with many children and grandchildren, and Joe had nearly recovered from his wound. It would be a lot of mouths to feed, but Fiona didn't care. This family had been with Will practically since he had arrived in America, and it would mean a lot to him for them to be here.

Fergus had promised to come, saying he might be bringing one of the McDowell girls he'd become sweet on if her mama would let her go on this special day.

Yes, she thought as she rolled out dough for an apple pie, it would be a happy enough Christmas. But there was a hole in her heart, too. Three of her children would not be with her.

* * *

Christmas day dawned clear and bright and promised to be one of those warm winter days that happened in the valley. Fiona was glad because it would mean the children could play outside. By noon, the final preparations were made, and just in time, too, as the Patersons rolled into the farm, steering their wagon and horses carefully through the entrance between the field and farmhouse, avoiding the ditch and abatis that remained in place.

Fiona had not told Will of their upcoming visit, and she watched him break into a huge smile when he saw his old friends come in, bearing food and fiddles. Fiona thought she might cry. It would indeed be a good Christmas for Will.

After the feast and lively conversation, at first mundane talk about the weather and crops but then it turned to the continuing conflicts. Wanting to avoid this sorrowful topic, Fiona brought out Will's fiddle and handed it to him. At this signal, some of the Patersons went for their instruments, and Fiona tucked her own fiddle beneath her chin and struck the first chord. She called the tune, and the merriment began. Mary and Jake took to dancing, stepping in place for lack of room, and others soon joined them.

One of the Paterson grandchildren took up a couple of spoons and beat a rhythm, another added the sound of broomstraw scraping the washboard. Alicia ducked out and went to her cabin, returning with her *ngoni*, and the *ceilidh* went into full swing.

No one inside the cabin heard the approaching riders, but one of the small children who had been playing outside ran through the door crying out, "They's coming!" The music stopped immediately, and Fiona reached for her rifle, as did the Paterson men. She stepped to the door, expecting to find trouble on her doorstep.

Instead, she found Cass, Jeannette, Maura with little T.J., and another man. It was Fiona's turn to be surprised, and she covered her mouth with her hand as her children dismounted and ran to her.

It was now the finest Christmas ever.

* * *

The stranger who was with them was introduced as Peter Eddelman, a young, brawny man with blond hair and blue eyes. His people had come from Germany, he told the rest of the family when they gathered later that night after the Patersons had gone home. The Eddlemans had farms in Pennsylvania, but some had come down the Old Wagon Road into Virginia and North Carolina. "I decided," he said, "to travel west to the tail end of Virginia and find land and have a farm for myself..." Then he looked pointedly at Maura. "...and whoever else I might meet up with out here." Peter had come to fight Patrick Ferguson as one of

Colonel Campbell's men. He'd met Cass and Jeannette, and through them, Maura. "I'm hoping your daughter and her son will become my family out here."

It was a quiet time after all the ruckus of the day, and the family sat by the fire, listening to the crackle of the wood. At Peter's statement, Fiona looked up at Maura, seated next to the very big, very white German. She looked small and dusky, but her expression, as usual, was inscrutable. T.J. had been put to bed. Could a big, blond German take on a little dark-skinned Indian child, Fiona wondered.

"Are you asking to marry Maura?" Fiona asked bluntly. From the corner of her eye, she saw Will shift in his chair, ill at ease at her forthright inquiry. But she wanted to know.

"If she will have me," he replied, looking directly into Fiona's eyes and not blinking.

"But that is her decision."

"Is this what you want, Maura?" Fiona smiled tenderly at her daughter, who like herself, had known the life of an Indian wife. Being the wife of a German man would be far different, Fiona figured.

"We have talked about it," Maura said quietly. "I'm considering it."

A very Cherokee woman's answer, Fiona thought and smiled inwardly. "You know it is your decision, and yours only."

With that, the conversation lulled again, and they sat in awkward silence, until Cass spoke up.

"You know, Ma, and Pa Will," he said, looking at them in turn. "I told you once I wasn't likely to ever settle down. Too restless to be a good husband to any woman." He then turned his gaze on Jeannette. "Until I found one as restless as I am."

Jeannette gave him the kind of smile only lovers share, and Fiona knew what was coming. Cass went on. "You remember you once told me, Pa, that you'd married a girl who you'd grown up with like she was your sister, only she wasn't."

A fond glint lit Will's eye. "Aye, that I did, son."

"Well, uh, Jeannette's not my blood sister, and, well, she and I want to get married."

It was indeed a day of surprises. Silence once again filled the room for a long moment as Fiona and Will considered this new bombshell. Jeannette had changed so much from the flighty, flirty girl always looking for a husband. She was tall, and strong, and a fighter, just like Cass.

Fiona had thought she might never marry again.

Fiona looked at Will. Will looked at Fiona. Then a slow smile began to make its way across Will's face, reaching his eyes and beyond. "If you children are asking for my blessing, you have it."

"And mine," Fiona said. She was reminded of something Quella had told her on her wedding day. One must take happiness when and where one can.

Cass reached out and took Jeannette's hand. "There's something more we need to tell you," he said, his face growing somber. "All of us. We've decided to move over to Kaintuck."

* * *

January 6, 1781

The Overmountain family, as Fiona was now calling them, stayed to celebrate "Old Christmas," the day they knew as Christmas before the English changed their calendar. Many of the families on the frontier still observed Christmas on this day. Some, like Fiona's family, decided to make a fortnight of celebrations between the two dates, with parties and festivities in between they called "breaking up Christmas."

But this Old Christmas was sacred in more ways than one, for today both Maura and Jeannette would be wed, one to her big German fellow, the other to one who once she considered to be her brother. Life on the frontier, Fiona thought with a smile, required flexibility.

Fergus had ridden back to Salisbury and found a magistrate who was willing to come to perform the ceremonies, as Jeannette would have nothing to do with a parson or a religious ceremony. Although it had been less than two weeks since Fiona had thrown the big Christmas surprise for Will, the cabin was once again filled, this time not only with the Paterson family, but with McDowells, Davidsons, Alexanders, and even John Carson, neighbors who had heard about the unusual event and traveled to wish the newlyweds—all four of them—well.

The wars had been too much with them all, and they seemed hungry for a reason to celebrate the life and the freedom they were fighting for. After the ceremonies, the merriment broke out, accompanied by a goodly amount of Will's liquid corn and some apple brandy brought by Hunting John and Annie. Music filled the cabin and spilled out the front door where a light snow was beginning to fall.

Fiona looked upon the scene with mixed emotions. She was happy for the young people, of course. But she was saddened by the knowledge that on the morrow, they would depart for the newly opened land in Kaintuck. Land still disputed by the Indians. Land that Dragging Canoe had vowed would be had at a bloody price. Their moving to a new land and the promise of freedom was an opportunity for them, but Fiona knew that finding freedom sometimes came at a terrible price. Her own journeys to freedom had been difficult, and she doubted theirs would be any easier. She wondered if she would ever see them again.

On the eve of their departure, she was suddenly struck how it must have been for her Da and Granny that last night before she left for the New World. Today's celebration, she thought, was very much like the one they had held for her.

It was, very much, an American wake.

BIBLIOGRAPHY

Alderman, Pat, *The Overmountain Men*, Johnson City, TN: Overmountain Press, 1986.

Bartram, William, *Travels of William Bartram*, edited by Mark Van Doren. New York: Dover Publications, 1955.

Bassett, John Spencer, *The Regulators of North Carolina*, Trinity College, NC, 1894.

Conley, Robert J., *Cherokee Dragon*. Norman, OK: University of Oklahoma Press, 2000.

Dixon, Max, *The Wataugans*. Johnson City, TN: Overmountain Press, 1989.

Duncan, Barbara, collector and editor, *Living Stories of the Cherokee*. Chapel Hill, NC: The University of North Carolina Press, 1998.

Fink, Paul M., "Jacob Brown of Nolichucky." Tennessee Historical Quarterly, Vol. 1. No. 1, Sept. 1962.

Furbee, Mary R., *Wild Rose-Nancy Ward and the Cherokee Nation*. Greensboro, NC: Morgan Reynolds Publishers, Inc., 2002.

Lee, E. Lawrence, *Indian Wars in North Carolina*, 1663-1763. Raleigh, NC: Office of Archives & History, North Carolina Department of Cultural Resources, 2011.

Maas, John R., *The French & Indian War in North Carolina*. Charleston, SC: The History Press, 2013.

McCrumb, Sharyn, *Kings Mountain*, New York: Thomas Dunne Books, St. Martin's Press, 2013.

Mooney, James, *Myths of the Cherokee*. New York: Dover Publications, 1995. (Reprint of Government Printing Office edition, 1900.)

Morgan, Robert, *Boone, A Biography*, Chapel Hill, NC: Algonquin Books of Chapel Hill, 2008.

Ritchie, Fiona, and Doug Orr, *Wayfaring Strangers-The Musical Voyage from Scotland and Ulster to Appalachia*. Chapel Hill, NC: The University of North Carolina Press, 2014.

Shames, Susan P., *The Old Plantation-The Artist Revealed.* Williamsburg, VA: The Colonial Williamsburg Foundation, 2010.

Swann, Anne Landis, *The Other Side of the River.* Kearney, NE: Morris Publishing, 2010.

Swisher, James K., *The Revolutionary War in the Southern Back Country.* Gretna, LA: Pelican Publishing Company, 2008.

The Junior League of Charleston, Inc., *Charleston Receipts.* Memphis, TN: Starr Toof Cookbook Division, 1950.

Timberlake, Henry, *Memoirs.* Signal Mountain, TN: Mountain Press, 2001 (reprint of original work, 1762.)

Woodward, Grace Steele, *The Cherokees.* Norman, OK: University of Oklahoma Press, 1963.